A VISIT WITH ROSALIND

**Other Apple paperbacks
you will enjoy:**

The Lancelot Closes at Five
by Marjorie Weinman Sharmat

Rich Mitch
by Marjorie Weinman Sharmat

Just Tell Me When We're Dead!
by Eth Clifford

Help! I'm a Prisoner in the Library
by Eth Clifford

Tough-Luck Karen
by Johanna Hurwitz

The Friendship Pact
by Susan Beth Pfeffer

A VISIT WITH ROSALIND

Marjorie Weinman Sharmat

AN
APPLE
PAPERBACK

SCHOLASTIC INC.
New York Toronto London Auckland Sydney

ISBN 0-590-42618-4

12 11 10 9 8 7 6 5 4 3 2 1   8 9/8 0 1 2 3/9

Printed in the U.S.A.   .   28

First Scholastic printing, November 1989

For Daddy and Uncle Ned
and for Weinman Brothers
Happy 50th

And I want to thank my sister, Rosalind,
for her resourcefulness and her
travels on the Portland scene,
which were of invaluable help.

A VISIT WITH ROSALIND

1

I was waiting for the mail the day I got the invitation. I really didn't expect any letters, but when I'm bored I do things like comb my hair every hour or read stories I've already read or watch for the mailman. We had two men on our route — Lynden, the main deliverer, and somebody short and fat who looked hot carrying the mail, even in the middle of winter. Lynden always wore thick white socks which I could see from a distance, and since I am interested in fashion, my opinion is that they didn't go with his uniform at all. But they made him look more like a mailman *person* and less like just a mailman. Anyway, I watched him come down the street, and when he got to my house he handed me the mail and flashed a smile as bright white as his socks.

"A letter from your friend Rosalind," he said. "It smells terrific."

Lynden was also nosy, as you can tell. I wondered if he had ever noticed the letters I got from

Shh . . . Secrets Magazine. They keep pestering me to subscribe. I think they got my name from a cereal company I sent a box top to, which was a dirty trick on the part of the cereal company.

Maybe Lynden noticed Roz's letter because she drenched it with perfume as usual, and perfumed stationery announces itself. It also smells up all the mail near it. My family is the only one ever to get a mortage notice from the Chase Manhattan Bank reeking of "Meadow Violet."

I thanked Lynden for the mail, and looked through it. Roz's letter was the only one for me. But it was enough. I opened it quickly. Roz had lived next door to me for three years and we had been best friends for almost all that time. We didn't say we were best friends. We really *were*. *Are*, as a matter of fact, even though she moved to Portland, Maine, which is farther away than I want to think about.

I will give an example of our friendship. I am terrible awful in gym. I don't see why a person who will grow up to be a fashion designer has to also be able to do a high jump. But there I was in gym, trying to do a jump in an obstacle course and I tripped over myself. This is very difficult to do if you *try* to do it. Along came Roz, who was the star of stars in gym, and she tripped over *herself*. On purpose. I never forgot that. She has also kept all my secrets — I *know* she has — and to this day she is the only kid who knows I have trouble counting change correctly, I swim like a sack of lead and a few other things about myself which I'd rather not mention. Roz told me that I'd outgrow these problems, and she named a few famous people who started out dumb in a subject and ended up an expert. "Wait," she said. "Your time will come."

Not only did Roz have all this sympathy for my problems, but she had plenty of sympathy left over. Once she told me the secret of what she did with some of her allowance, but I'm keeping it a secret. All I'll say is that if there were more Roz's in the world, people begging in the streets would become financially independent. And she is also very big on stray cats and wounded birds. She takes them all in. If every stray cat were given Roz's address, there wouldn't be a homeless cat left anywhere.

I opened her letter. It had a few perfume stains on it, but I could read it.

Dear Anna,

You are now smelling "Desert Dawn." I made it myself out of the dregs of my mother's old perfumes "Desert Me Not" and "Daring Dawn." What do you think of the name and what do you think of the aroma? I know what I think. Great!!!!!

Anyway, please excuse me for not answering your last letter immediately if not sooner and please excuse the spots which I just now made on this stationery.

That takes care of the excusing, and now I have GOOD NEWS!!!! Wait till you hear this. I can invite you to come visit me. My mother says so. You can come anytime, but I am inviting you for right now — spring vacation. From Sunday to Sunday. Tell your mother and then tell me immediately if not sooner if you can come. I would have invited you more in advance, but I didn't know more in advance that I could invite you.

I won't write any news in this letter because I will see you very soon and we will have a GREAT time and I am looking forward to it, and so are you I bet.

Remember IMMEDIATELY IF NOT SOONER let me know.

Your best friend no matter where I live,
                                    Rosalind

It was one of my favorite all-time letters. I had been hoping for four months — ever since Roz moved away — for an invitation to visit her. I had already gotten permission from my mother to go whenever I was invited. Since Roz lived so far away, I hoped I could take a plane. I had flown on planes twice before, when my whole family went to Florida to recover from miserable colds that wouldn't go away up north no matter what we tried.

I ran to tell my mother. She was busy sniffing a bill from Con Edison which smelled of "Desert Dawn."

"Did you get a letter from Rosalind or is this another public relations stunt from Con Edison?" she asked.

My mother is a regular guy, if a mother can qualify for that description. Her idea of motherly isn't home-baked bread or receiving one perfect rose on Mother's Day or speeches about love. She wears dungarees constantly, she is terrific at most sports, she swears now and then, and her number-one hobby is writing letters to famous people, including baseball teams, telling them what they are doing wrong and occasionally what they are doing right. Her favorite person to write to is the President of the United States. She usually encloses clippings from newspapers that she thinks he might have missed reading. She has never gotten a direct reply from him, and her last letter to him (which I read over her shoulder) said, "Why haven't you answered me? I know you're home."

Anyway, that's my mother. As you can see, we are opposites. Me, the non-athlete of non-athletes, will become a leading fashion expert. (If I become famous enough, my mother might write me a letter telling me I should design more dungarees and fewer dresses, and I will answer her letter no matter how busy I am.)

I never got a chance to answer her Con Edison question. She said, "Rosalind invited you to visit her *immediately if not sooner*."

My mother had a good memory for Roz's writing style. (Roz never said that expression, she only wrote it. I wonder why people have habits of writing words they don't say, and saying words they don't write.) My mother was also quite good at mind reading or guess-work, whichever would apply in this case.

I nodded.

"Well," said my mother, "you can go immediately if not sooner."

I didn't even have to remind my mother that she had promised I could go. "By plane?" I asked in a tiny voice.

"Public transportation in this country is going to the dogs. In fact, it qualifies as lousy," said my mother. "Lord, how many times have I told the President that. But the planes are pretty safe and they're fast, and the airlines always answer my letters, which is more than I can say for the railroads. You can call Rosalind after five tonight, when the rates go down, to tell her you can come."

Somewhere in my mother's answer I think she

meant I could take a plane. I hugged her.

I ran to my room to look over my clothes — my *wardrobe*. Anybody who knows anything about clothes and traveling knows you should pack clothes that don't wrinkle and that wash easily and dry fast. The only clothes I had that fitted that category were a pair of nylon gloves with a hole in the left thumb. My mother believed in sturdy clothes that could thrive on the whack of an iron and the gyrations of a washing machine.

I took my faded blue and green plaid suitcase from the back of my closet and started to pack. I made a mental note that someday I would design a more exciting looking suitcase. What I didn't know then was that adventure can come wrapped in faded blue and green plaid.

2

My mother called the airline, I called Roz after five o'clock, and the next afternoon my mother and father and I were at LaGuardia Airport checking in me and my suitcase for the nonstop flight to Portland, Maine. My suitcase went with the rest of the suitcases, and my parents and I went into a passenger lounge to wait for the boarding announcement. I was lucky to get a last-minute plane reservation (which mine practically was), especially on a Sunday.

But some of this wasn't as simple as it sounds. My parents had almost backed out of my mother's promise that I could go. When I called Roz the night before, I found that she had left an important detail out of her letter. It seems that her mother and father had gone to Bangor, Maine, to visit Roz's aunt, and Gilda the maid would be in charge of us. Roz's father would return on Sunday night, but he would be at work most of the time I'd be visiting. Roz had convinced her parents that now would be a perfect time for me to visit so she wouldn't be lonesome.

I cannot mention Gilda the maid without explaining Gilda the maid. Gilda had worked for Roz's family like forever. When she went to work for them she was poor, but somewhere along the way she had inherited a huge amount of money from a rich uncle who had some oil wells in Texas. (Up until that time I didn't believe that uncles with Texas oil wells actually existed, like Santa Claus.) Anyway, after Gilda got the money, she immediately told Roz's parents that she was leaving. She left, but she didn't stay away for long. A few days later she showed up at Roz's house and announced that Roz's family couldn't get along without her. They invited her in and she's been there ever since.

Gilda got on the phone and my mother got on the phone, and Gilda told my mother that she would watch Roz and me "like a Texas hawk." I don't know if a Texas hawk is different from any other kind of hawk, or even if there are hawks in Texas, but Gilda liked to mention that state whenever possible. She also told my mother that Roz would be terribly disappointed if I didn't come. Then Roz butted in on the conversation and said, *"Please."*

So that's how it got worked out.

My mother was gazing around the lounge, and

my father was gazing at me. He had given up his Sunday afternoon nap to see me off. I was touched, because he really needs that rest. "A Sunday afternoon nap is my prescription for myself," he always said. He's a very busy doctor, a five-magazine doctor I'd say. He's so busy his patients have time to go through at least five magazines while they wait in his reception room. I am his "Valentine," "Cupcake," "Sweetheart," "Sugar" and "Honey." These are direct quotes. He is full of nicknames. He calls my mother "Sport" and she grins like a batter who broke a tie game in the last inning.

My mother recognized a famous person in the lounge — an actress to whom she had written several fan letters, and who had sent her an autographed picture.

"Her handwriting is for the birds," said my mother. "But she can light up any stage. Try to sit next to her. She's probably full of stories. Find out if she was born on Majorca like she claims or in Brooklyn like Aunt Fannie heard."

"It's nicer sitting next to a nobody," I said, "and trying to guess his occupation and why he's traveling."

"Sugar, you've got a real inquisitive mind. That's a sign of intelligence," said my father.

I glanced at the people in the lounge. Some of

them were there to see people off, and the others would be flying with me. There wasn't anybody as young as me, and that made me feel big. There were a couple of babies, but they didn't know what it was all about, and besides, they weren't traveling alone.

The boarding announcement came. We lined up at the boarding gate.

"Call us collect whenever you want," said my mother. "Remember us to Rosalind and her father and Gilda. Help Gilda with the dishes even though they're part of her job. Don't drink any perfume by mistake. Rosalind puts it in Coke bottles, remember."

My father said, "Take care of yourself, Sweetheart. Sit by a window so we can wave to you."

The man at the gate took my ticket. I kissed my parents fast and then I rushed across the field to the plane. Inside the plane a stewardess greeted me. Someday I would also like to design stewardess' uniforms, but I didn't tell her that. I said hello in a very friendly way, right after she said hello to me in a very friendly way. I walked down the aisle, looking for a seat by a window. They were all taken. So I stood in the aisle, wondering where to sit, while people tried to get by me.

I finally picked a little old woman and sat down

beside her. She smiled, almost gratefully, as if she had half expected me to sit on her lap and was relieved when I didn't.

"Is this your first flight?" she asked.

"My third," I said. "I've already been to Florida and back."

"Your third," she said. "My, you *are* brave. This is my first and last flight. If I could have gotten a satisfactory bus connection, I wouldn't be here. Did you read about that horrible plane crash in the Himalayas?"

I had sat down next to the Nervous Nellie of all Nervous Nellies. Up until then, the only similar trick that fate had played on me was to place me in the same classroom as Slugger Schultz, who poked me regularly.

I looked past her out the window. I could see my mother talking to the actress, who I guess had been seeing somebody off. So I couldn't have chosen the actress to sit beside, anyway.

The No Smoking and Fasten Your Seat Belt signs went on. The plane's engines started up. I waved to my parents, but I didn't think they could see me. They seemed to be waving at space in general. The lady next to me asked the stewardess to check her seat belt for her. Then the lady turned her head about, trying to see if anyone was smoking. "It's terrible to cheat at a time like this," she whispered.

12

The plane started down the runway. Fast, faster. It was the fastest I could ever remember going, even on the Florida planes. And then we were in the air, and everything below was getting smaller and smaller. The lady beside me was staring out the window as if her eyes were bolts fastening the plane to the sky. She knew what she was doing: if she took her eyes away, the plane would surely drop. I didn't want to disturb her important work, so I busied myself in a quiet way by reading the instructions that I found in the seat pocket in front of me. I had read the same things on my trip to Florida, but I refreshed my memory on how to possibly save my life in case of major trouble and how to throw up neatly in case of minor trouble.

Suddenly the lady turned to me. "I hope you don't mind my saying that you're using your noodle, my dear. Reading that literature *now* could save your life."

This was the second compliment about my intelligence in less than an hour, if compliments from your own father count. I thought I should do something with my "real inquisitive mind," so I began to wonder if the lady had an occupation besides Safety Expert, Self-Employed. She went on talking. "My name is Thistle," she said. "*Miss* Thistle. And whom do I have the pleasure of sitting beside?"

I told her my name was Anna. My mother had told me never to tell my last name to strangers because it was like giving away too much too soon. I noticed that adults have regulations for themselves, too. They only give their last names.

Miss Thistle told me that her fifth cousin on her mother's side was also named Anna. "Life is full of coincidences, my dear." Then she went back to her eye work.

I looked out the window, too. There were white clouds against a blue sky. Lynden's color scheme.

A stewardess came around taking orders for tea, coffee, or soda. I ordered soda. Miss Thistle didn't order anything. She was asleep. Keeping an airplane flying, even in your mind, can exhaust you. I was going to order tea, and save it for her. But maybe she would think that was a silly thing to do, and why should I spoil that perfect record I had with her?

Miss Thistle slept on. I drank my soda, and then I closed my eyes, too. Suddenly — at least it seemed suddenly — a stewardess was announcing that we were about to land. Miss Thistle stayed asleep. Her seat belt was still fastened, so there was no reason to disturb her. I tried to get a glimpse of Roz's city through the window, but I was afraid of leaning on Miss Thistle. Then we were down, and the plane slowly came to a stop. Miss Thistle woke up.

"We've landed," I said extremely cheerfully. "We made it."

"Did we?" She looked out the window. "Yes, we did. Ground is so beautiful, isn't it? Well, good-by, my dear, and I do hope you'll keep reading instructions. You'll live longer."

Miss Thistle slid over me and hustled off the plane. I got off the plane, half looking where I was going and half looking for Roz.

And there she was, she and Gilda, standing in a crowd at a long cyclone fence. I rushed toward her shouting, "Hi!" We grabbed each other and hugged hard. Roz has a sweet, sweet face and I had missed seeing that face and everything else about her. Gilda shook my hand. She had more hair and more teeth than I remembered. She asked how my family was and if my mother was still keeping the U.S. Post Office in business.

I took out a little gift I had picked out at LaGuardia. It was a plastic napkin holder with a picture of the Empire State Building. When I grow up I'll design a better one, but for seventy-nine cents this wasn't bad. Naturally I planned to send Roz a gift when I got back home, but my mother thought it would be practically immoral to arrive empty-handed.

"Just what I always wanted," said Roz. Gilda had told her a long time ago that she couldn't go wrong saying this whenever she received a gift, and I know for a fact that when Gilda got the news of her inheritance, these were the first words out of Gilda's mouth. Roz added, "Our old napkin holder is all beat up."

We walked to the moving platform where the suitcases were being unloaded. One of the first ones to appear was a faded blue and green plaid. I grabbed it and Roz grabbed it from me and Gilda grabbed it from Roz.

The suitcase was enjoying more popularity with us than it deserved considering the fact that it wasn't mine. If I had waited a few minutes I would have seen an even more faded blue and green plaid suitcase — *my* suitcase — arrive on the platform. But we walked off, with Gilda enthusiastically carrying the possessions of a complete stranger.

3

I liked Roz's house. It was white, with dark green shutters, and it had a screened front porch. It was different from the one she had next door to me. In some ways it was bigger, and in some ways it wasn't as big. That's about the only way I can explain it. It gave me an odd feeling to watch her and Gilda moving about in this strange house, especially when I remembered their old kitchen where I had spent so much time. It had seemed to belong to them, and it should have been movable like them and gone where they went.

I recognized some of Roz's old stray cats, and she had some new ones. She now owned seven, which was more than her New York average.

There was so much to say. I wondered if any visit would be long enough to get in all the subjects we had to talk about. On the ride from the airport, Roz had been busy pointing out places she thought might interest me, or places where somebody she knew lived or places that reminded her of New York. The biggest question in my mind got answered on that ride, though. Roz pointed out the house where her closest friend in Portland lived. "She's nice," said Roz. "But she's not you. You're my best friend."

"And you're mine," I said.

Sometimes when somebody moves far away, or they die, they get to be more important in people's minds than they were before. But it can work in the opposite way. They can fade away. Well, I hadn't faded for Roz, and she hadn't faded for me.

Roz took me up to her bedroom. There were twin beds in it. Although Roz is an only child, she has tons of cousins who visit her. She let me pick which bed I wanted. I knew which one was her regular bed. I could tell by the cat pillow on it. I picked the other bed.

Roz was waiting for me to notice a large piece of paper taped to the wall over her dresser. It had pink and yellow flowers painted around a message:

Anna
Welcome
to Portland, Maine
and my house

I knew that Gilda didn't like anything stuck on walls because the wallpaper or paint might get damaged, so Roz really must have begged to be allowed to tape up that piece of paper.

"I couldn't have designed a better sign if I worked forever on it," I said. Since Roz knew about my designing ability, this was top praise for her work.

"Do you want to tour the neighborhood first or unpack?" she asked. "It won't be much of a tour. Gilda is setting up limits."

I didn't know when clothing wrinkles passed the point of no return. Were seven or eight hours of wrinkling worse than five? I decided to unpack first on the theory I had just made up that wrinkles wrinkle more as time goes by. I opened the suitcase.

The clothes inside were neat and smooth. They were very attractive, too. If you liked men's clothes.

Roz said, "So *that's* what the girls are wearing back in New York now. I left just in time. I prefer dresses myself."

"Your best friend is a dope," I said. "I picked up the wrong suitcase."

"As long as you were doing that, you should have gotten one filled with money," said Roz. "When you return it they hand you a big reward, if they're not stingy, and everyone gives you much

19

more praise than you deserve, just for being honest. I'm honest all the time and nobody notices. Nickels and dimes, nobody notices."

"Okay," I said, "I'll remember that the next time I take a suitcase by mistake. But right now I've got a case full of men's clothes. You know, I wonder why someone with nice clothes like these would have a suitcase as dumpy looking as mine. Feel the material of this jacket. Glorious."

As I fingered the jacket, I also fingered a piece of paper sticking out of the pocket. It looked positively untidy the way it stuck out. I took it out of the pocket and laid it on the jacket.

"There's something written on it," said Roz. "What does it say?"

"It says none of our business," I answered. But I glanced at the note. After seeing the first sentence, I had to read on.

The note said:

Memo from S.H.

  Get rid of Miss P.P.T. as best you can
  Destroy her if necessary
  On May 3rd replace her with Sabrina

I showed the note to Roz. She read it, and said real fast, "You're-right-it's-none-of-our-business-close-the-suitcase-quick-and-let's-return-it-to-the-airport-and-get-yours."

"What if whoever owns this case took mine?" I asked. "What if I have to meet him or something?"

"Simple," said Roz. "Why do you think they teach you to run obstacle courses in gym? To prepare you for a situation like this. You go up to this guy, give him his suitcase, grab yours, and *run*. If there's a fence or something in the way, you can handle it. It's probably been a long time since he took gym. Say, who do you suppose he is, anyway?"

I looked through the whole suitcase. I was hoping to find more notes, clues, any information at all. I found out what brand of toothbrush, toothpaste, shaving cream and shampoo the man used. I found three handkerchiefs with the monogram S.H. in dark blue. I found out that the man was fat, because his clothes were large-sized. I noticed that all the suits had the label WYMAN BROTHERS, PORTLAND, MAINE.

"That's the best store in town," said Roz. "And the biggest."

"Well, he's S.H. That's for sure," I said. "That means he's the writer of the note, not the receiver."

"Do you think he's a murderer?" asked Roz. "Or maybe he just hires people to do the dirty work, and is that ever dirty work. Ugh." She walked away from the suitcase.

"If we could only forget that we saw the note," she said. "But let's face it, we can't. This Miss P.P.T. may be in real danger. So now we have to do something about it because — because, well, we have to."

I was thinking back to my plane trip. The suitcase belonged to Mr. S.H., a passenger. I wished I had been more observant. I had wasted my time with Miss Thistle when I could have been . . . sitting next to a master criminal. On second thought, hooray for Miss Thistle and that gorgeous seat beside her.

Had any of the passengers looked like criminals? As a future designer who is very much aware of looks, I happen to believe that there is no one special way for a criminal to look. Years ago there was. Criminals in the old movies on TV often showed up with a slouchy hat and upturned collar, a hand in a pocket (closed over an invisible gun), a cigar in the mouth, and menacing eyebrows. I think that every self-respecting crook in those days at least tried to look a little like this. Nowadays a lot of the criminals I see in newspapers dress in an ordinary way, especially the big criminals as it seemed Mr. S.H. was, and they look super respectable. Planes are full of super respectable looking men.

"What are you thinking about?" asked Roz.

Roz was looking for ideas, ideas like what do we do now.

"We'd better return this suitcase to the airport right away," I said. "And get my suitcase if it's there. And we'll try to get the name of the person who owns this case."

"Say, I just had a creepy thought," said Roz. "S.H. means quiet. Do you suppose it's a code for "Keep this under your hat, don't tell a soul, OR ELSE?"

I said, "Ever hear of a hand-embroidered code, with *curlicues* to boot?"

"Sure," said Roz. "Just now."

"The monogram on the handkerchief is a work of art, not of intrigue," I said. "Believe me, *I* know. Now let's fix up this suitcase."

"Hey, I just thought of something," said Roz. "A few years ago there were some murders out west where the murderer always left a souvenir behind with his initials on it. Sometimes it was a card, sometimes a piece of paper, and sometimes a *handkerchief*. The newspapers called him 'The Monogram Murderer.' He was never caught. Maybe he moved east and is getting started all over again."

"What were his initials?"

"Oh, boy," said Roz. "I can't remember everything. But wait, there was something about them.

Now I know. They were S.S. I remember thinking they were Slugger Schultz's initials."

"Slugger Schultz isn't *that* bad," I said. "You know, S.S. is fifty percent like S.H. Do you think it means anything?"

"We won't find out just standing here and talking," said Roz.

Roz and I tried to arrange the contents of the suitcase to look just as they had when I opened it. It was a lot of work and we couldn't remember exactly how the clothes had been placed. Finally we gave up. We made sure that the top suit looked neat, and I put the note back just where I had found it. *That* position I remembered.

I carried the suitcase downstairs. Roz walked several steps in front of me. She wanted as little as possible to do with the suitcase.

Gilda was in the kitchen. She looked up when she heard Roz and me and the suitcase. I guess we had frightened looks on our faces or maybe I was carrying the case in an unusual way, for she said, "What's the matter with you girls? You act as if there's a dead body in that case."

Thanks to Gilda, I realized that the situation could have been a whole lot worse.

4

We told Gilda that I had accidentally taken the wrong suitcase. Before we told her, we laughed at her little joke. Ha-ha.

She drove us back to the airport. She was the official chauffeur for my visit. She had enrolled for driving lessons right after she had inherited her money, but she had never gotten around to buying her own car. The car belonged to Roz's family. Gilda didn't mind being called a chauffeur, Roz whispered, because Roz's mother was also a chauffeur. "But if this were a limousine and she had to wear a uniform, she'd quit."

At the airport Roz and I started to get out of the car, but Gilda said that she'd go and take care of everything. She always wanted to do for Roz what Roz wanted to do for herself. She was like that when Roz's mother was around, too, but she really took over when Roz's mother was away. Roz once said, "When I'm fifty years old, Gilda will be about ninety, and she'll still try to run my life." I told Gilda that I was the only one who knew exactly what my case looked like so I should be the one to go. (My credentials for recognizing my own case were not terribly good, but nobody mentioned that.) I suggested that Roz go with me, and that Gilda keep the motor running so we could make a fast getaway. That was a nutty thing for me to say, and not very funny, but Gilda laughed. She owed me a laugh from her dead-body joke.

Roz and I took the suitcase up to a counter where a pleasant man in an airline uniform asked, "May I help you?"

"This suitcase isn't mine," I said. "Do you have one like it that's mine?"

"Do you mean that you have someone else's suitcase?" he asked, and smiled.

"That's what I mean," I said. "Is there maybe one hanging around the airport that looks like this?"

"There's maybe one hanging around the baggage room that looks like it," the man said, still smiling. "And it can be claimed if you have the baggage check for it."

I fished in my purse and found the baggage check, which was attached to the folder containing the copy of my airplane ticket. I handed it to the man.

"I'll be back in a minute," he said. In a minute he was back with a faded blue and green plaid suitcase. I felt waves of ownership passing between it and me. It was mine.

"The gentleman who owns the case you took will be delighted to hear that it's been returned." The man smiled. "He's telephoned twice inquiring about it."

"How do you know he's a gentleman?" asked Roz.

The man smiled. He always smiled.

"What's his name?" I asked point-blank. I had planned to be crafty and cautious and indirect, and it was a shock to find that my own self could be undependable. But I felt pretty cocky with this man who smiled all the time. Either he wanted to or he had to, but whichever it was, he was too busy smiling to switch gears and get suspicious.

"Why do you want to know his name?" he asked from behind his smile.

Roz said quickly, "My friend would like to thank the man for not taking her suitcase by mistake."

Roz's reply was very good, in fact excellent, if you didn't think about it for more than a second or so. But if you gave it more than a couple of seconds' thought, you'd realize that what she said was absolutely ridiculous.

The man said, "What a lovely thought, little lady. I have his name right here. Let's see. It's Mr. Sherman High. His telephone number is 722–6652."

"Is that spelled 'high' like way up or 'Hi' like hello?" asked Roz.

"High like high in the sky, little lady."

Roz scribbled the name and number on a piece of paper. Roz always carries pencil and paper the way some people always carry combs or tissues or lemon drops. "Thanks loads," she said.

"My pleasure, little lady," the man replied.

I took my suitcase, and Roz and I walked away giggling.

"Get that name," said Roz. "Sherman High. Sounds like a school. Sherman High, Sherman High, rah! rah! rah!" Then she sang, "Sherman High, we will ever be true to you, loyal to old Sherman High."

We roared. We really did. We were actually having f-u-n fun. That's what I had come to visit Roz for. That's what she had invited me for. We looked at each other in a kind of happy, surprised way. Fun *was* still possible.

Gilda was waiting with the motor running. "Good," she said. "You got your case. You're sure that's the right one?"

"Couldn't be surer," I said. I patted it. It reminded me of a droopy faithful dog that had come home to its master.

Gilda sat us down for supper the minute we got home. Roz's father arrived at about the same time. So Roz and I had no chance for a private conversation except for a few whispers in the back of the car.

Roz's father said, "You've really grown, Anna."

I didn't know what to say back. There are certain rules in greeting people you haven't seen for a long time, and I was just in the midst of learning them. I think they go this way: An adult is supposed to tell a child that she has changed, that she's grown. The child then feels that she's accomplished something. But she is not supposed to tell the adult that *he* had changed. In fact, she would do well to say, "You haven't changed a bit." An adult accomplishes something by managing to look the same year after year.

I said a safe and honest, "I'm very happy to see you."

The meal was delicious. I was careful to finish every last bit of food. I knew that Gilda was a stickler about that. On her list of possible sins, leaving food on a plate ranked very high.

"How about my treating you girls to a movie tonight?" Roz's father asked. Gilda looked at him to see if she was included. Ladies over thirty love being called a girl, if it's said with a straight face.

Roz said, "We're too tired, Daddy. Today has been — too much. Anna and I are going upstairs and relax." Roz kicked me under the table. Kicking under a table is a speedy form of communication which I happen to know adults use also.

Relax was certainly a peculiar word to describe what Roz and I did upstairs. We schemed and planned and discussed until we really were tired. Now that we had S. H.'s name and telephone number, we didn't know what to do about it. Finally Roz said, "Too much talk. Too little action." She picked up the telephone receiver. She had an extension phone in her room which was something she hadn't had in her other house. She dialed 722–6652. I leaned over and put my ear close to the receiver, so that we could both hear.

A woman answered, "Hello."

"Oh, hello," said Roz. "May I speak to Mr. High, please?"

"He isn't home yet," said the woman. "He's working late at the store."

"What store?" asked Roz.

"Who is calling please?" asked the woman.

I was wondering when she'd get around to that question. Roz hung up. It wasn't polite, but it was sensible.

"What were you trying to do?" I asked.

"I was just trying to get information," said Roz. "And I did. He works at a store."

"A store that's open on Sunday? I wonder what store?"

"That was *my* question," said Roz. "But the woman wouldn't tell me."

"What would you have done if Sherman High

had been home and answered the phone?"

"I haven't the vaguest idea," said Roz. "But sometimes when I do something right on the spot without knowing in advance what I'm going to do, well it works out terrific."

I snapped my fingers. "We forgot something, we two geniuses. We can look up Mr. High-in-the-Sky in the phone book and see where he lives." Giving Sherman High a nickname made him seem a little less terrifying.

"You are so right," said Roz. She put the phone book on her bed and started flipping pages. She flipped her cat pillow on its side by mistake, and it lay there stiff, maybe like a future victim of Sherman High. "I can't find his name," said Roz. "Here — you look. I don't trust myself."

I couldn't find the name either. "He must have an unlisted number," I said. "Did you know that you have to pay the telephone company for *not* listing your name in the book?"

"So he has money," said Roz. "But what do you expect? People in his line of work *always* have money. Maybe we should just plain call the police. Maybe we should have turned the suitcase over to them."

"Maybe yes, maybe no," I said. "He hasn't really *done* anything bad that we know about. Only his plans are fatal. And they won't be fatal until May 3rd. That's a few weeks away."

31

"But you're only here for a week," said Roz. "And then I'll be stuck with this mess. That poor Miss P.P.T. I wouldn't want to be in her shoes. This Sabrina must be prettier and younger. Criminals go for surface stuff like that. Hey, do you suppose that Miss P.P.T. is really a *Mrs.* and maybe she's Mrs. High-in-the-Sky? I bet she scrubs floors for him, and waits on him hand and foot, and this is the thanks she gets."

"How can his wife have T for a last initial when his last initial is H?" I asked.

"Right again," said Roz. "I'm tired. To be continued tomorrow, okay?"

"To be continued tomorrow," I said.

Roz took her cat pillow off her bed, sat it up carefully on a chair, stroked its whiskers, and then turned back the covers of her bed. I was in bed before her. I didn't have a cat pillow, and I was very, very tired.

5

The next morning Roz and I woke up hungry. We said, "Hi, I'm starved," to each other and that was the extent of our conversation before breakfast. If was just about the extent of our conversation *at* breakfast because Gilda was in a presiding mood and breakfast gave her something to preside over. She had our day planned for us and she was going over the details. She felt that little details properly taken care of led to big successes. For example, she was a collector of trading stamps. I've watched her sticking them in stamp books with such energy you'd think she was pasting toward some world-shaking goal, but her goal was actually an artificial orange tree, one foot high, which you can get for 2¼ books. I have also observed her stopping a run in her stocking, which I think is a small problem. She put colorless nail polish on the end of the run as if she were crushing an invading monster in his tracks. And a fingerprint on the wall was a defeated enemy when she got rid of it with Mr. Clean.

So Gilda had our day planned detail by detail. "You're going shopping," she said. "I've mapped out the route." Gilda showed us her itinerary of stores we would visit. One of them was Wyman Brothers.

"Perfect," I said to Roz when Gilda was out of hearing distance. "We can look for suits with the Wyman Brothers label. When we find the label, we can start asking the salesman questions. A salesman might remember Sherman High."

"Since this is Portland, he might," said Roz. "In New York they don't remember you unless you have two heads and one of them is green."

Roz and I were in a good mood, thinking about our shopping trip and our plans. But then we learned that Gilda was going along to take care of any problems and details. What she didn't know was that she was the problem. Roz and I wanted to be alone.

But the matter was settled. The court of last resort had adjourned: Roz's father had gone to work. He had been leaving just as we came down for breakfast. He had put us "in Gilda's capable hands" and walked out the door.

Roz and I went upstairs to get dressed. Roz put on a new dress. At least it was new to me. "Pretty," I said. I put on the dress that had best survived being packed. "Pretty, too," said Roz. It wasn't.

"Would Gilda get very upset if we lost her while we were shopping?" I asked.

"Upset is putting it mildly," said Roz. "She'll give herself fifteen minutes of searching time. Then she'll call the police. She wasn't that way before she got money. On second thought, I'm glad you didn't find a suitcase full of money if money makes a person that kooky. Even the reward might affect my mind."

"Well, somehow I'm going to stop and look at men's suits," I said. "Even if I have to faint in the men's department."

We had to wait for Gilda to straighten up the house and get ready, so we spent some time with Roz's cats. Roz introduced me to the new ones by name. She always named her cats after counties. The New York cats were Westchester, Suffolk, and Sullivan. The newcomers were Androscoggin, Aroostook, Cumberland, and Penobscot. Then Roz took me to the basement, which was her perfume workshop. She was making a perfume with real lime, mint, and sassafras oil and she was naming it after herself. The perfume after that, a combination of buttermilk, chopped rose petals, and crushed dandelions, she would name after me. She had dozens of Coke bottles lined up. She liked their shape. But she never washed out the bottles before she used them. A bottle isn't really empty until it's washed out, and so all of Roz's perfumes had warm Coke as an ingredient.

Gilda called down, "Time to close the perfume factory, my Texas lambs. We're off."

Gilda drove us to town, of course. This was my first visit to the main part of Portland because our trip from the airport had been through the outskirts, which were mostly residential.

We passed a statue of Henry Wadsworth Longfellow, who was born in Portland and grew up there. He was a sitting statue and Roz told me that kids sometimes managed to sit on his lap even though it was very high from the ground, and they weren't supposed to do it. "Handsome, isn't he?" said Roz. "Did you know that Portland is the largest city in Maine and it has one of the best harbors on the Atlantic Ocean and it was settled in 1632 but was burned down — four times I think — in attacks? Portland is real historical, except that I haven't heard of anybody famous sleeping here."

"How about me? I asked.

"Funny, funny," said Roz.

Gilda heard me. She laughed. She really liked my jokes.

Gilda's itinerary was: small stores first, big stores later. It fitted her personality. In the first shop we visited, I bought an adorable yellow scarf with green porcupines crawling around the border. I bought an identical one for Roz except that her porcupines were gray. Roz objected and said that I really shouldn't do it, but I did it. I was glad that I had brought along fifteen dollars from home.

We went from store to store until finally we got to the biggest store in town — Wyman Brothers. "Famous for labels on Sherman High's suits," I whispered to Roz.

Wyman Brothers was having a 50th Anniversary celebration. At each entrance to the store there was a large picture of Nathan and Harry Wyman, the founders and heads of Wyman Brothers. They looked nice and successful in a kind sort of way, and they didn't have that smiling-down-on-you-from-way-above expression I've seen in photographs of other executives. (Naturally, I cannot be a designer of faces, but that doesn't stop me from being an analyzer. For the record, I have dark brown hair, very long, very large dark brown eyes, and even teeth.)

There was a biography under their pictures. I read the last paragraph first because I've found that last paragraphs often have more colorful information than first paragraphs. The last lines said the Nathan Wyman played the mandolin in his spare time, and Harry Wyman practiced hypnotism. Then I read the first paragraph and learned that they were born in a little town in

Poland and came to this country as kids. They sold shoelaces on the sidewalks of New York, and later earned six dollars a week in Memphis, Tennessee, and then moved to Portland where they started Wyman Brothers in the back room of a dressmaker supply store. My mother would say that they had "made good." My mother and I once had a talk on that subject. I was curious how a person could make good if he were born rich. My mother said he could go into politics.

I never got to read the middle paragraphs because Gilda, who was not a biography reader, tapped me on the shoulder and said, "We're going in."

Inside the store, which was like Macy's in miniature, there were streamers and posters and special decorations everywhere. Each salesperson was wearing a carnation (pink for the ladies, red for the men). They were also wearing tiny cards with their names written in, and 50TH ANNIVERSARY printed on top. Young salesgirls in pink and red floor-sweeping costumes were handing out fliers describing special sales. The store was crowded. I've always wondered whether this kind of celebration peps up salespeople like a regular party would or knocks them out like having too many guests would.

The men's department was at the front of the

store. Roz and I stopped. Gilda dashed ahead to look at some jewelry in the next department. She had forgotten about her Texas hawk-watch.

"She's crazy for jewelry," said Roz. "She won't miss us."

Roz and I walked up to a rack of suits. "Look for the Wyman Brothers label," I said.

Roz and I started poking through the suits. Suddenly I heard a voice that seemed to come from directly above me. It *was* directly above me. A very tall salesman had claimed property rights to the air just over my head. He bent over me. "Do you want to buy a suit?" he asked.

Already he wasn't cooperative. He should have asked, "May I help you?"

"Well, that all depends," I said. "We're looking for suits with the Wyman Brothers label."

"Do you want to buy a suit with the Wyman Brothers label?"

"That all depends, too," said Roz. "We'd like to see them."

The salesman looked at Roz and me suspiciously. Then he said, "The Wyman Brothers suits are on the rack over there, little lady." People were forever calling Roz "little lady."

The salesman's head left the space above my head and the rest of him went with it. Roz and I followed.

The Wyman Brothers suits had their own rack to themselves. "These are pretty," I said. "Aren't they, Roz?"

"Oh, sure," said Roz.

"Could you tell me more about them?" I asked.

The salesman sprang to life as people do when they are asked a question they are especially qualified to answer.

"The Wyman Brothers suits," he said, "come in a varity of styles, fabrics, and colors. All the fabrics are imported and the tailoring is superior. The suits range in price from $179.99 to $249.99."

"Thank you," I said. The salesman looked disappointed, as if he thought his description deserved more than a thank you.

I was thinking, if the suits are *that* expensive, salespeople would probably remember who bought them. Although stores like to refer to anyone who walks in the door as a "valued customer," people who spend a lot of money actually are.

"Do you have many customers for these suits?" I asked.

The salesman's chin jutted out over me. He said in a sharp voice. "Yes. Now are you one of them or are you not?"

I figured I had about one minute left — maybe less — before he exploded.

I said, "I hear that Mr. Sherman High buys his suits here."

"Where else?" said the salesman. "Are you buying a suit for him?"

"No," said Roz. "My friend would like to thank him for not taking her suitcase by mistake." Roz was all confidence.

"Are you and your friend interested in buying a suit, little lady? Answer yes or no."

"I usually don't believe in straight yes or no answers," said Roz. "But if I believed in them, I'd say no."

"Then why don't you two go be pests in the girls' department? You can be more efficient pests there. You can try on the clothes. Good day."

The salesman walked away in a huff. Roz felt sorry for him, but I didn't. After all, his job was to wait on the public, *any* public. "What atrocious manners," I said.

"But he was sort of helpful," said Roz.

I nodded. "If we only knew what he meant by 'where else.' "

"I've got it," said Roz. "I've got it, got it, got it. Last night when I phoned Sherman High's house, we found out that he works in a store. Now he would probably buy his suits in the store where he worked, if they sold them. And they do. He works at Wyman Brothers. Where else?"

"But you forgot," I said. "Wyman Brothers isn't open on Sunday. Wait, I've got it, got it, got it. Sherman High has a high-paying — hey, get that, *high*-paying — job with Wyman Brothers. He's an executive, a big shot. Big shots often work on Sunday. Big shots . . ."

"Please, not that last expression," said Roz. "Ugh."

6

Gilda was summoning us to the jewelry department, so we joined her. "Don't wander
off like that," she said. "It's too hard for me to
keep track of you. I'm not the Texas Rangers, you
know." She held up a necklace with a rhinestone
elephant hanging from it. "What do you girls think
of this?" she asked. Then she answered, "Never
mind. It's my decision."

Roz whispered to me, "She's really in a fog
lately. It will take her an hour to decide if she
wants this necklace. In that hour, you and I could
look for Sherman High."

Roz and I were standing behind Gilda. Very
quietly, we started to walk away. Gilda was saying something, but I couldn't hear what it was.
"She's not talking *to* us, she's talking *at* us," said
Roz, when we were several feet away. "She
doesn't expect an answer. She won't miss us — I
hope. Let's go up the stairs."

A stairway was just ahead. Halfway up the

stairs, we looked down. Gilda was still gazing at the to-buy-or-not-to-buy elephant.

We got to the second floor. Roz stopped. "Are we going to ask for Sherman High or look around for him?"

"Let's look first," I said. "If we ask, the word might get around that we're hunting for him. He's fat, I can tell by his clothes, and he also might have an initialed handkerchief sticking out of his pocket. And maybe he'll be wearing an anniversary card with his name on it. There are mostly women around, so that makes our job easier."

"I see a fat man over there," said Roz.

Roz pointed to a fat man who seemed to be examining price tags on children's coats. "He could be a customer," I said. "But he's fat enough to be High-in-the-Sky."

Roz and I walked over to children's coats and stood next to the man. He kept on looking at price tags. He wasn't wearing an anniversary card, but there was a handkerchief sticking out of his pocket. It looked as if it had been pulled out, and then put back any old way. If there was a monogram on it, it was buried down in the pocket.

Roz was also looking at his handkerchief. She sneezed. "Do you have a handkerchief?" she asked me.

"No," I said. "No, I don't have a handkerchief. A handkerchief is something I don't have."

"That's too bad," she said, "because I really need one." Roz sneezed again. Roz's athletic ability extended up to her nose. If somebody ever said to me, "Sneeze," I couldn't. If somebody said. "Sneeze and I'll give you a million dollars," I couldn't. If somebody said, "Sneeze and you'll become the most famous designer who ever lived," I couldn't. But Roz could sneeze just on the hope of borrowing a used handkerchief.

The man moved on. I didn't blame him. Now if he got a cold, he would blame it on the sneezing girl who had been next to him in children's coats. He didn't know he had seen a performance that some people might stand in line for. Roz followed after him, but it was a lost cause. The two things that people hate to lend the most are handkerchiefs and toothbrushes, and the more Roz seemed to need a handkerchief, the less likely it was that the man would lend it.

I had another idea. I had read somewhere that people are always alert to the sound of their own name. For example, if a person is in a room with a lot of people and there is a lot of noise, that person might still hear his name being mentioned from across the room, even if he couldn't hear any other words. So if I mentioned the name Sherman in a conversation, this man might turn my way if his name was Sherman. And he wouldn't suspect that I thought *his* name was Sherman.

I said to Roz, "I was studying the Civil War just before spring vacation and did you know that William Tecumseh *Sherman* was a Confederate general?"

The man turned around. He had a dignified face. He seemed to be the kind of man who would tip his hat if he were wearing one.

"I overheard your remark," he said, "and I believe that all the history books would be in disagreement with it. Sherman was a Union general. He lived from 1820 to 1891. He was a graduate of West Point and he succeeded Grant as commander of the peace army in 1869. Your friend has a wretched cold. May I offer some tissues?"

The man handed Roz some tissues which she put to her talented nose. The man would have made a great historian, but a terrible doctor.

He said, "Good day," and he sort of bowed and walked away.

"That's Mr. Courtly-Portly," I said to Roz. "And he's not Sherman High." I knew he couldn't be Sherman High, just like I knew that the sky was blue, grass was green, and William Tecumseh Sherman was a Union general.

"Oh, golly, here comes trouble," said Roz.

"Trouble Gilda" was coming up the escalator. Since Gilda's face is just about the same whether she'd mad or not mad, I couldn't tell if she was mad. But I could certainly guess that she was.

"Let's get out of here," I said. "Take a coat and run to a dressing room. Don't run too fast or you'll look like a thief."

Roz and I each grabbed coats and made for a dressing room. Fortunately, the dressing rooms were not between us and Gilda. We went into the first empty one. I closed the curtain. There were two chairs, and we sat on them. We heard a saleswoman making the rounds. "Put your coat on," I said to Roz. Roz tried and so did I, but the coats were so small we couldn't get our arms through the sleeves.

The saleswoman opened the curtain. I said, "It's such a bore trying to pick out something for someone else. This would probably be perfect for my little cousin in kindergarten, but then again, how can I be sure? Does this store do alterations? Never mind, my cousin is such a brat that if I pick out red, she'll insist on brown, and if I get a round collar, she'll say she wants it pointed. I think we'd better forget it for the time being. Some day I'll bribe her with a lollipop, and get her to try on her own clothes. Thank you ever so much for your help."

I handed the saleswoman a coat, and Roz handed her a coat. She took them and she stood there, as rigid and silent as a real coat rack. Roz and I walked out.

Gilda wasn't in sight. "Gilda goes from left to

right, just like she goes from small to big," said Roz. "So she'll probably be looking for us in sportswear, which is across the floor. We can go down the elevator and we'll be back in jewelry before her."

We had to wait for the elevator. We kept watching for Gilda while we waited.

"The elevator operator must be camping out on the third floor," I said, "Look at the floor pointer. It's been at three long enough to pick up an army."

"Union or Confederate?" said Roz. "What was that General Sherman business anyway? I know it had something to do with Sherman High but — "

"Never mind. Here's the elevator," I said. The elevator door opened. The elevator had not been worth waiting for. Gilda was one of the passengers.

I said to Roz, "You remembered left and right, but you forgot top and bottom."

"If I remembered everything, I'd be a genius," said Roz. "And then you wouldn't be able to stand me."

"Come in," said Gilda.

I wondered if she was going to make a scene in the elevator. She crossed her arms. She was.

"Don't you ever run away from home again," she said.

"Home?" I asked.

"When you're with me, *I'm* home," said Gilda.

"You might as well have packed a knapsack."

It was a short scene. We got to the first floor, and Gilda marched ahead of us to the jewelry counter.

"We got off easy," I said.

"Gilda doesn't believe in carrying on when she's mad," said Roz. "She says her piece and that's it. She calls it 'short and sour.' "

Gilda picked up the elephant necklace. She took up right where she had left off. "I just can't decide," she said. "His trunk bothers me. If only he didn't have that flashy trunk." She covered the elephant's trunk with her finger. "Well, an elephant just isn't an elephant without his trunk, even a rhinestone trunk."

"Would you like the necklace?" A saleslady appeared from around the other side of the counter. She looked familiar. Even without her seat belt and her quivering and her safety warnings, I recognized Miss Thistle.

"Hi," I said. "Remember me? From the airplane."

"Why, hello, my dear," she said. "Of course I remember you. You have the same name as my fifth cousin. I don't recall which fifth cousin, but it will come to me. Don't help me. It's comforting to meet on the ground, isn't it?"

Then Miss Thistle turned to Gilda, who was still trying to decide if she wanted the elephant, trunk and all. "He's very popular with us," said Miss Thistle.

If I were the saleslady I would have said, "An elephant never forgets, and you'll never forget the compliments you'll get when you wear this glamorous necklace."

Miss Thistle raised her hand. "I remember your name. It's Anna. I'm like this elephant. An elephant never forgets, you know."

I said, "And you're Miss Thistle. We both remembered."

"But my dear, did you remember it or read it?" Miss Thistle pointed to the little card she was wearing:

50th Anniversary

Prudence Priscilla Thistle

Maybe it didn't mean anything at all — and maybe it did: Miss Thistle's initials were P.P.T.

7

Gilda put the necklace back onto the counter. "I'll think about it," she said.

"Would you like me to hold it aside for you?" asked Miss Thistle. "I'll be glad to."

"No, I'll take my chances," said Gilda. "Thanks for your help."

"Anytime," said Miss Thistle. She turned to me. "It was lovely seeing you again, Anna. Do keep your feet on the ground."

"I will, and you take care of yourself, Miss Thistle. I really mean that." Now Nervous Nellie was *my* name. Was Miss Thistle the target of Sherman High? There wasn't any time to think about it because Gilda was marching toward the door. "Time to eat," she said. "Looking at the elephant made me hungry."

"For rhinestone peanuts?" I asked.

Gilda laughed. Roz giggled. And why not? It was a great joke.

Outside Wyman Brothers, Gilda turned left and

marched to a restaurant that had two unlighted neon fish swimming in unlighted neon waves in the front window. Inside the restaurant there were wooden fish swimming on walls, paper fish swimming on napkins, and cardborad fish swimming on menus. The restaurant was named In the Swim Seafood House.

"Fish is king here," said Gilda. "But you can order other kinds of food."

I began to read the menu. After I read all the foods, I started reading prices. A waitress came to the table, and Gilda said, "Broiled mackerel and iced tea," and Roz said, "Hamburger with French fries," and I still was reading prices. As I mentioned before, I have this problem counting change — even before I get the change. I couldn't afford to spend more than 2 dollars for lunch and still have enough money left for shopping. Included in the 2 dollars would be a tip for the waitress which should be about 20 percent of a bill, and the tax — which I knew from buying the scarves — was 6 percent of a bill. If I could subtract the tip and the tax from 2 dollars, I could spend the rest on food. But how could I know what the tip and tax would be unless I knew how much the food was? So I had to make trial runs with different foods. A grilled cheese sandwich was 60 cents and a glass of milk was 15 cents and a dish of French fries was 35 cents. That added up to

$1.10. And 20 percent plus 6 percent of the $1.10 plus the $1.10 subtracted from $2.00 was — "

"Gilda's treating us," said Roz. She knew my problem. I ordered the grilled cheese sandwich, the milk, and the French fries. I had already invested a lot of time and effort in that combination.

Now that my financial problem was solved, I went back to thinking about Miss Thistle, Miss Prudence Priscilla Thistle, Miss P.P.T. I was dying to tell Roz about my discovery, but Gilda was there.

"I think I'll go comb my hair," I said. I kicked Roz under the table.

"I think I'll go comb my hair, too," said Roz.

"Good idea," said Gilda.

The three of us went to the ladies' room.

As soon as we got back to our table, the waitress came along with our food.

"Annie, do you remember the old times when we used to play restaurant?" asked Roz.

"Sure," I said. "We each took turns being the eater and the waitress. The waitress set the table with a knife, fork, and spoon whether the eater was going to use them all or not. The eater sat down and ordered from a menu that had been written in advance. After the eater had eaten, the waitress brought a check, which also had been made out in advance. After the eater got the check, she stood up and took the waitress's apron and became the waitress. The ex-waitress sat down and became the eater. The check was always correct because it was always the same no matter what the eater ordered: twenty-five cents plus twenty-five cents plus fifty cents equals one dollar plus one dollar tip for the waitress because the service was so good. The restaurant owner never got any tax money because he wasn't in the game."

"I don't get it," said Gilda. "What did you actually eat?"

"Bread and water," said Roz.

"Sounds like jail," said Gilda.

Jail made me think of Sherman High. And then I was back thinking about Miss P.P.T. And then I had an idea.

"Say, Roz, I thought of a new menu for our game. Could I borrow your pencil and paper?"

"Sure," said Roz. "But don't you think we've outgrown that game?"

"This is a real up-to-date menu," I said. "A *to-day* menu, you might say."

I wrote something on the paper and handed it to Roz: "That Miss Thistle at the jewelry counter. Did you catch her initials? P.P.T. ! ! ! ! !"

"That *is* a tasty tidbit," said Roz. "But we should talk about it before it's all gobbled up."

"I agree," I said.

Roz and I thought and ate. Gilda just ate. The

waitress came to take orders for dessert. Roz ordered a strawberry sundae. Gilda ordered a "Sea Shell," which the waitress described as looking like a Chinese fortune cookie and tasting like "a fisherman's dream." As I read the list of desserts, I noticed a sentence at the bottom of the menu. It said, "You are invited to inspect our kitchen."

I ordered a chocolate sundae and said, "Look at this invitation. We're invited to go to the kitchen."

"Nonsense," said Gilda. "They don't mean it."

"It says we're invited," I insisted.

Gilda said, "It's like 'come and see me sometime.' That's not an invitation either. But 'come and see me at three o'clock next Saturday,' *that's* an invitation."

"I want to see the kitchen, don't you, Roz?" Naturally I kicked her.

"Wild horses couldn't keep me away," said Roz.

"Well, I don't," said Gilda. "If I'm going to get thrown out of a place, it'll be a fancier place than a fish kitchen."

Roz and I walked to the back of the restaurant very slowly. "Do you think Miss Thistle is really *the* Miss P.P.T.?" she asked.

"Yes, because she and High-in-the-Sky work in the same store. They were on the same plane, too, but they didn't sit together. They might possibly hate each other, and High-in-the-Sky plans to do something about it. Miss Thistle wouldn't harm a fly. Anyway she's for keeping anything up that flies." I laughed. Roz didn't quite get the joke. "Shouldn't we warn Miss Thistle?" she asked.

"I say no. I say we should be positive about everything first. If we warn Miss Thistle, she could drop on the spot, believe me."

"I believe you," said Roz. "Now can we go back to the table?"

We were almost at the kitchen. I looked back. Gilda was watching us.

"We have to go into the kitchen," I said.

We walked through swinging doors into a hot, fishy kitchen.

"A great big kettle of fish," said Roz. "Well, we inspected. Let's go."

We turned to go.

A plump man in a chef's uniform came rushing up to us. "Were you looking for the ladies' room?"

"No," said Roz. "We came to inspect the kitchen and we did and now we're leaving."

"Vistors!" shouted the chef. "Hey, boys, they came to inspect the kitchen." The chef's right hand and left hand clutched each other eagerly, as if they were having a reunion. "For three years now, we've had that invitation on our menus. And how many people do you think have come? Exactly six. Six in three years. This is an occasion. Come sit. Eat! Inspect!"

Some of the men gathered around us, handing out bits of food, mostly cooked fish. "If we had known about this earlier we could have had a free meal," I whispered to Roz. "But we'd have to be just plain crazy about fish."

"As you can see, all our equipment is modern, the latest," said the chef. "And notice how clean everything is." He waved his arms about. "And fresh. The fish over there were caught today. *Today*. How's that for fresh?"

A man was removing a newspaper covering a container full of fish and ice. Then he began putting the fish into a huge refrigerator. It was kind of interesting to watch, like being backstage. Presenting The Fish Follies, starring Felix Flounder and Hortense Halibut.

The man finished putting the fish into the refrigerator. He pushed the newspaper into a carton filled with refuse. One corner of the paper stuck out. I noticed the name WYMAN BROTHERS on an advertisement. I was really tuned into the name. The ad had a drawing of a beautiful young woman wearing a smashing outfit. The woman's name was spelled out in large letters S–A–B–R–I–N–A.

Poking out of a corner of a carton in a fish-filled kitchen was not exactly where I expected to get my first clue about Sabrina. There was no convenient table to kick Roz under. I said, "Say, Roz, have you read all the news that's fit to print and

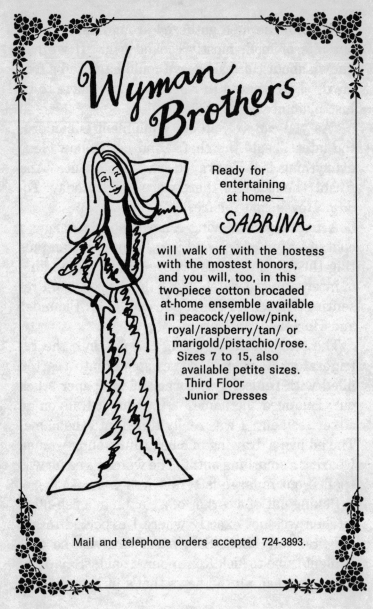

wrap fish in *and get clues from?*" I pointed to the newspaper.

"You girls are interested in everything, aren't you?" said the chef.

Roz looked at the ad. "A drawing of Sabrina," she whispered. "And see, I was right. She is young and pretty, if the drawing looks like her."

We read the ad. We had to lean over the carton to do it, but neither of us wanted to touch the fishy newspaper. The newspaper was a week old — the one item in the room that wasn't fresh.

"Oh, I might have known," said the chef. "You're after the clothing ads."

"We always like to inspect the whole works," said Roz. "But we really must be leaving now. We don't want to overstay our welcome. We had a lovely time and thank you for everything."

"Come in anytime, little lady. And tell your friends about us, too. We cater children's birthday parties."

"My age group doesn't go for that," said Roz, "but I'll tell the little kids I know."

I said, "Thanks, chef." That was about all there was left to say after Roz had said her good-mannered good-by.

Outside the kitchen we stopped. "Roz, do you have any old newspapers?"

"Tons," said Roz. "Downstairs with my perfumes. I pour over them so I won't mess up the table and the floor."

"Wonderful. You and I are going to do some reading. About Sabrina. If we can find her in the newspapers."

"What about Miss P. P. T. and Sherman High?" said Roz. "All of a sudden we're rich with clues. Just this morning, we were poor. Now we're like an army that can advance on three fronts. Or we're like — "

I interrupted. "We're like two girls who have to stop talking because here comes Gilda."

"Girls, girls, your sundaes are soup. Strawberry and chocolate soup. What were you doing in there, inspecting inch by inch, scale by scale, fin by fin?"

Sundae soup doesn't taste bad at all, Roz and I found out, but you lose a lot of ice cream and syrup.

"We're going home," Gilda announced. "We're too tired to shop any more today."

Gilda had made it easy for us to know what front to advance on. She simply took away our power to make a decision. We were going home, home to the Newspaper-Sabrina front.

We were home in twenty minutes flat. That included paying the bill, walking to the car and stopping for gas, a bottle of milk, and four red lights. In her own way, Gilda had talent.

8

Roz had enough old newspapers near the furnace to burn down Portland for the fourth time. I knew our friendship was strong enough for me to criticize her for creating "hazardous conditions," as the safety ads say.

"It's Gilda's fault," she explained. "She's a saver. You know, pins, old ice-cream cartons, used gift wrappings and, of course, string. I only need a few newspapers but she keeps adding to them. We're fixing her. The Boy Scouts are having a newspaper drive next Thursday, and my father is putting all these papers out at the curb at seven in the morning, which is pickup time. At that very minute, if she sticks to schedule — and she usually does — Gilda will be in the shower yodeling 'The Eyes of Texas Are Upon You.' So chalk up one good deed and one less 'hazardous condition' as of next Thursday. Meanwhile, be glad I've got these papers to go through. As you know, it isn't every house that has such a fabulous collection."

Roz took one pile of papers and I took another. "Let's stick to business," I said. "We're only interested in Wyman Brothers ads, and we're looking for Sabrina."

Whenever I read a newspaper I'm afraid I'll miss something if I don't at least glance over everything. I had to force myself to single out the Wyman Brothers ads and not peek at anything else.

"I found one," said Roz. "From two weeks ago. 'Sabrina at Breakfast.' Listen to this. 'Breakfast with Sabrina is a delicious experience as Sabrina makes a fetching entrance wearing a knee-lenth black and white velveteen housecoat with detachable inserts of red and black patent leather around the neckline and hem. Matching red and black patent leather slippers complete the costume.' "

Roz sighed. "Some life this Sabrina leads. Hey, how does this sound? Rosalind makes a fetching entrance at breakfast wearing flannel pajamas ripped at the left knee and a bathrobe handed down from three older cousins. Matching torn slippers complete the costume."

"You sound irresistible," I said. "I'll buy you. Now keep on looking. There must be other ads."

There were others, similar to the two we had seen. "Sabrina at the Beach," "Sabrina at Work," "Sabrina on Vacation." Sabrina here, Sabrina there, Sabrina everywhere. We put them in one pile.

"Don't you ever read ads?" I asked Roz. "How could you have missed all of these when you got your newspapers?"

Roz looked angry. "I read perfume ads," she said. "I'm entitled to my specialty, and you're entitled to yours."

"I'm sorry," I said.

That was the nearest we came to having a fight while I was in Portland. And I don't think it was very near.

"Okay," said Roz, "since you're sorry, I'll tell you about my discovery. First of all, have *you* made any discoveries?"

"Nope."

"Okay, I'll tell you mine. All the Sabrina ads are in this month's and last month's papers. She's not in any of the Wyman Brothers ads in the older papers. That means she's kind of new. Maybe Sherman High only recently made her acquaintance, as the saying goes. Or — "

"Or what?"

"Or maybe it doesn't matter how new or old she is. Maybe she's just a drawing and that's it," said Roz. "It's possible, right?"

"*Im*possible," I said. "If she's only a drawing, how could she replace Miss P.P.T., like the note said? Miss P.P.T. is Miss Thistle."

"But what if Miss P.P.T. *isn't* Miss Thistle? What if *she's* a drawing?" asked Roz.

"If she's a drawing, go find her," I said. "We saw the older ads. They didn't feature any special drawing or name. And I'll tell you something. There would *never* be a drawing of Miss P.P.T. Customers can't identify with an initialed lady, or a three-names lady."

So Sabrina lives and breathes," said Roz.

"And up to May 3rd, Miss P.P.T. does the same," I said. "I wish I knew what plans High-in-the-Sky has for Sabrina. And I wish I knew just who Sabrina is."

"Well, I made a discovery about her past," said Roz. "You figure out her future."

"Thanks a lot," I said. "May I please have next week's newspapers."

"I'll give you today's," said Roz. "That's the best I can do." She ran upstairs and then ran down with *The Portland Evening Express.* "It just came," she said. "It says evening but it usually comes in the afternoon."

"Let's make bets," I said. "Sabrina at the circus. How's that?"

"How about Sabrina in the fish kitchen?" said Roz. "We know she was there."

I started turning pages. I stopped suddenly. "Hey, Roz, listen to this. Sabrina is getting her own Sabrina Shop in Wyman Brothers on May 3rd! Look at this ad."

The ad had "Sabrina on the Tennis Courts," and below it in swirling letters:

Wyman Brothers
Is Pleased to Announce
That Sabrina Will Have
Her Own Sabrina Shop
On Our Third Floor
Starting May 3.

"Anna the Discoverer. If I had the power, I would knight you or give you a medal or whatever I had the power to do. But asking questions drains me of all my powers. Like do you suppose Sherman is seeing to it that Sabrina has a shop? Hey, sounds like did Peter Piper pick a peck of pickled peppers? Do you suppose Sabrina works somewhere in the store? Or does Sherman know her from the outside? Where does Miss Thistle fit in? Is Sabrina getting her shop over Miss Thistle's dead body — good-by, Thistle, hello, Sabrina?"

"For the answer to these and other questions, don't ask me," I said. "But we could get some answers if it weren't for General Gilda. We could ask around Wyman Brothers for Sherman High and Sabrina."

"But he could find us before we find him," said Roz. "So maybe General Gilda's doing us a favor without knowing it."

"Good point," I said. "And fortunately I have another plan. We'll do just what my mother would do. Write a letter. To Wyman Brothers. We'll ask for information about Sabrina. We'll pretend that we're customers who like the ads. In a way, we are."

I was glad we had a plan, that we were taking some small step forward. Maybe this was how Gilda felt pasting in her trading stamps. I thought of a bad joke: how many stamps do you need to get a criminal?

Roz supplied the pencil and paper, and we both supplied the words. We crossed out, we erased, we added and subtracted words. Finally we had a letter we both liked. Roz copied it in ink. Her penmanship is better than mine. The letter said:

Dear Mr. Wyman Brothers,

Happy 50th anniversary to you and many of them. We are satisfied customers of your store. We saw your ads about Sabrina in the newspaper and they are very interesting. Could you please tell us everything about Sabrina? Please answer soon. We are in a hurry to know.

Thank you in advance.

Your satisfied customers,

Miss Anna Richardson & Miss Rosalind Fox
133 Dartmouth Street
Portland, Maine 04103

Roz and I went downstairs to tell Gilda we were going to the mailbox. She was scrubbing the kitchen floor, so we stood outside the kitchen. Roz said, "We're going to the mailbox."

"All right," said Gilda. "I'll take you as soon as I finish this."

"I meant Annie and me," said Roz. "We have to get there before the next mail pickup. It's in fifteen minutes. Otherwise my letter won't get picked up until tomorrow."

"If somebody wants to hear from you, they'll still want to hear from you one day later. You two can't go without me. The mailbox is outside limits."

"Three blocks is outside limits?" said Roz.

"Yep. May as well be San Antonio, Texas. You can't go without me."

Roz and I walked away. "We *can* go without her," said Roz. "We'll just sneak out. That is, *I'll-*

sneak out, and you'll help me do it."

"How? She can see the front door and the back door from where she is."

"We'll get her away from where she is. You and Androscoggin and me. Come on down to the basement."

Androscoggin was asleep in the basement under the perfume table. "I knew he'd be in here," said Roz. "He really goes for this place." She woke him up. "He's the fastest of my cats. That's why I picked him for this job. I've got the letter in my pocket so I'm all set to leave. Your job is a cinch. Take Androscoggin and let him loose on the kitchen floor. It's still wet and he'll track it up. Gilda will go after him and I'll sneak out the front door. It's a mean trick to play on Gilda, but she treats me like a five-year-old."

Roz, Androscoggin, and I went upstairs. Roz walked toward the front door. I walked toward the kitchen, holding Androscoggin. I had a one-word excuse made up in advance, and as I let Androscoggin down at the kitchen entrance, I said it: "Oops!"

Androscoggin did not run through the kitchen. Instead he turned around and ran straight to the open front door where Roz was busy making what she thought was her escape. Gilda ran after Androscoggin. Roz had an excuse made up, too. "Just letting the cat out," she said.

"Of the bag," said Gilda. "You've got some kind of plot to get that letter mailed. Well, I'll help you. How's that?"

"Why, that's great," said Roz. "You'd stop your work to help us?"

"No, I wouldn't," said Gilda.

And she didn't. Roz and I really didn't mind too much washing the rest of the floor while Gilda went out to mail our letter, but when Gilda got back — the moment she walked in the front door — she started asking questions about the letter. "I saw it was to Wyman Brothers," she said. "Don't worry, I didn't open it. I read the envelope and I held it up to the light. That's fair. Opening the envelope, that's something else. That's a crime."

"Could you read any of the letter?" I asked.

"Nope," said Gilda. "The envelope was too thick. Thick envelopes take half the fun out of life."

I suddenly got an idea that when I returned to New York I would write a letter to Roz, telling her exactly what I thought of Gilda, and I would put it in a very thin envelope.

Gilda went to the kitchen to make supper. The floor wasn't quite dry, but Roz and I didn't wait around to hear about it. We went upstairs and closed the door. Now that we had done all we could for the time being, we put ourselves in low gear.

We spent the rest of the afternoon talking about neighborhoods — her old one, which is mine, of course, and her new one. I told her the latest about her old friends and unfriendly friends, including Slugger Schultz. I also gave her a definite invitation to visit me when summer vacation started. It wasn't a come-and-see-me-sometime invitation. It was as sincere as the restaurant's invitation to inspect the kitchen, and *that* was *sincere*.

At supper Roz told her father about the scarfs I had bought for her and for myself and about the rhinestone elephant Gilda had almost bought. "Does it eat rhinestone peanuts?" he asked.

Gilda and Roz laughed as if they had never heard a question like that before. It should not be one of life's great disappointments to find that an absolutely terrific joke you've made up has also been made up by someone else. But it hurts.

I was sort of in the mood for a movie that night, but Roz's father said the movie had changed and the new picture wasn't recommended for anyone under eighteen. There wasn't a movie in town that was. So Roz's father never got to take the "girls" to a movie, and Gilda never got to find out if she was one of them.

After supper I called my parents collect. I told them general news, that my plane trip was okay, that Roz and her father and Gilda were okay, and that I had gone shopping and that was okay, too. Over the long-distance telephone, it costs more money for things to be more than okay, and I wasn't sure what kind of investment my parents wanted to make in details. But I found out. My mother told me that the actress at the airport couldn't get a taxi so my mother and father gave her a ride to Forest Hills, which was on their way home anyway. My father also removed a splinter from the actress's finger, and she promised to send two tickets to her new show opening on Broadway. Then my mother said she was glad everything was okay with me and that the house was quiet without me. My father got on the phone and said the house was quiet without me and asked, "Whom did you sit with on the plane, Sweetheart?" I said, "Miss Prudence Priscilla Thistle" in a very definite way, as if I had certainly found the right person to sit with. My father said, "Fine, Sugar, I'm proud of you." I told him I'd call again soon and then I said good-by.

Roz and her father and I watched a movie on television. Gilda came into the room every time the movie got noisy, and left every time it quieted down. She liked action. My mother's actress had a part in the movie, and I thought that was quite a coincidence. I told Roz and her father and Gilda all about the splinter and Forest Hills and the tickets. "She's some actress," said Gilda. "She was born in Texas, you know."

The movie lasted until eleven, but Roz's father didn't watch till the end. Gilda called him away to show him a leaking pipe. "What, again? Our pipes are jinxed," he grumbled. That was the only time he grumbled during my visit.

Roz and I dragged ourselves upstairs and just about fell into bed. Portland could be more tiring than New York, but Roz and I were probably the only people in the world who knew that.

The next day began quietly. Gilda hardly said a word at breakfast. She had no plans for us. She said this would be our "day off." She sounded like an employer. Back upstairs after breakfast, I told Roz that we could also take a day off from the Sherman High business. "Nothing drastic will happen to Miss P.P.T. before May 3rd," I said. "We've got time. And our letter must have arrived at Wyman Brothers today. If they answer right away, we might hear tomorrow."

"Something drastic will happen to *me* before May 3rd," said Roz. "You'll go home and leave me to finish up."

"You worry too much," I said.

"Annie, if you'd worry more, I'd worry less," said Roz. She shrugged. "Change of subject. Want to go over to Libby's today? She wants to meet you."

Libby was that close friend of Roz's. I wanted to meet her, too. I was hoping to find something wrong with her, I think, but I didn't admit that to myself. After we were at Libby's house for a while, I realized there wasn't anything to find. In fact I liked Libby very much. Roz has good taste in friends. We spent all day there, including lunch. Gilda drove us over and Gilda picked us up, of course.

The day that began quietly ended quietly. After supper we watched television for an hour and then went to the basement to check on the progress of Roz's new perfume. It was progressing. It smelled like gumdrops. Roz purposely dropped a little on Sullivan and Cumberland, who were purring around. She said it improved their social life.

We went to Roz's room. When we were in bed I asked, "What time does the mail come?"

"Anytime between ten and one. Do you really think we'll get an answer as soon as tomorrow?"

"Let's sleep on the hope that we will," I said. And we did.

At a quarter to ten the next morning Roz and I went on a Mailman Watch. The weather was beautiful, so we watched outside on the front porch. We told Gilda that we wanted to air ourselves. She hadn't mentioned whether this was another day off, and we didn't bring up the subject. In a way, watching for a mailman was a kind of symbol of my visit. It had all started when I watched Lynden come down the street and hand me Roz's letter. Now I was back watching for a mailman again.

"Does he wear white socks?" I asked.

"Purple with orange polka dots and pink stripes," said Roz. "Honestly, how should I know what kind of socks the mailman wears? Who notices things like that?"

Roz got silence for an answer. She looked at me. "Oh, Annie, I'm sorry. You do."

Roz's mailman wore conservative navy blue socks. He showed up at twelve-thirty. He handed the mail to Roz. "Thank you, Richard," she said. She knew his name, if not his socks.

There were five pieces of mail. None of them was for us.

We spent the day looking forward to the next day. There wasn't anything else to do, anyway. Gilda was staying in, so Roz and I were staying in.

The next morning we went on our Mailman Watch at ten. Richard came at eleven-thirty. He had one piece of mail. It was for Roz and me. It was from Wyman Brothers.

9

We tore open the envelope. The letter was written on thick crinkly paper. I told myself that it wasn't the type of paper that would be sent to any old customer. The letter was from Nathan Wyman.

I said to Roz, "Imagine a busy man like that answering us personally and immediately."

"Maybe we wrote a crackerjack letter," said Roz.

"Someday I'm going to tell my mother about this," I said. "This is *her* specialty."

"Let's read it already," said Roz.

Dear Customers:

Thank you for your recent letter congratulating us on our fiftieth anniversary of service to the people of Portland. Letters from our customers are always welcome, and are read with great interest. We have been most pleased with the reception given Sabrina, and we feel that she represents today's fashion-conscious young woman. As you probably have read, because of the tremendous success of our newspaper campaign, commencing May 3rd Sabrina will have her own Sabrina Shop in our third-floor dress department. There Sabrina will be seen in the fashions featured in our newspaper advertising. If you would care to meet her in advance of the general public, we will be happy to arrange it whenever you are in the store. Please come to Room 302 on the third floor and ask for Mr. Sherman High, our promotion manager. Again, on behalf of my brother Harry and myself, thank you for your interest in Wyman Brothers.

With warmest wishes,
Nathan Wyman

NW:mws

Roz and I congratulated ourselves on our intelligence in writing to Wyman Brothers.

"This is our day," said Roz. "Now we know just where to find Sherman High. Some promotion manager, huh? Ugh."

"And we actually have an invitaion to meet him and Sabrina," I said. "This is the invitingest city. But we're not about to accept *this* invitation. We'll just browse around the third floor."

Roz looked worried. "Say, do you think Mr. and Mr. Wyman are in on Sherman's plans?"

"I certainly don't. I took a good look at their picture. Pictures can be very revealing to the trained eye. I could tell these were real gentlemen. After all, Mr. and Mr. Wyman can't know what all of their employees are up to. Employees can take two-hour coffee breaks, steal, sell business secrets to competitors — all kinds of dishonest things. I'm up on this stuff, you know, and that's what can happen when you run a big store. The Wyman brothers will be very grateful to us when we expose what probably is the rottenest apple on their store family tree."

"And just how do we get to the orchard?" asked Roz.

"It's almost lunchtime," I said. "We'll see what Gilda has cooked up — cooked up for activities, that is. After we find out what we have to escape from, we'll plan our escape."

At lunch Gilda said, "What was the name of that saleswoman in the jewelry department? The nervous one with the elephant memory?"

"Miss Thistle," I said.

Roz and I exchanged looks. Maybe this wasn't our day. Was Gilda on to something? Or had some terrible thing already happened to Miss Thistle and was it in the newspaper and had we missed it?

Gilda went on. "I've decided in favor of that rhinestone necklace. I'm going to buy it."

"Are we all going to Wyman Brothers today?" I asked.

Translated, that question meant, are you going to wreck our plans today, Gilda? If she went to Wyman Brothers with Roz and me and we got ourselves conveniently lost again, she would get us conveniently found fast, even if she had to personally marshal the store detectives for the search.

"I'm ordering it by phone," said Gilda. "I have to stay in this afternoon. The plumber's coming to fix the pipe."

Roz broke into a big smile and kicked me. I didn't think the news was *that* good. I was glad that Gilda had to stay home, but I wasn't, say, ecstatic, because it didn't solve the problem of Roz and me leaving.

Roz said to Gilda, "Before the plumber comes, could you drive Anna and me to the library? That would be a fun way to spend the afternoon. In the library."

Gilda gave Roz a puzzled look. So did I. "That library's so dusty it's one big sneeze from end to end," said Gilda. "Except where those wicked best sellers are. *They* move on and off the shelves so fast it keeps the dust away. I'll give you a ride if you leave soon. The plumber's due anytime after two-fifteen."

There was something going on that I didn't quite understand. Roz seemed to know exactly what she was doing. I knew only part of it. She had gotten us a ride to town. The library was just a few block's walk from Wyman Brothers. She had also gotten us an alibi of sorts for the afternoon. And Gilda had forgotten about her *outside limits*.

After lunch Roz and I went upstairs to get ready. I had told Gilda it would take five minutes. I had allotted Roz five minutes of explaining time. "What's going on?" I asked.

"The plumber is coming," said Roz. "The plumber is coming."

"Who do you think you are, Paul Revere? I mean, so what, the plumber's coming."

"So plenty," said Roz. "The plumber is — get this — Gilda's boyfriend. He's — how do you say it — sweet on her and she's sweet on him. She's plenty glad to get us out of the house. I knew she'd take us to the library. She might take us straight to Wyman Brothers, if we ask, but we'd better not."

"Do you know all of this or are you guessing?"

"Listen," said Roz. "In the past few weeks we've had leaking pipes, clogged pipes, broken pipes, rattling pipes and loose pipes. Gilda keeps asking me if I've been pouring my perfume mixtures into the drains, but that's just a cover-up for what she does to the pipes. She sabotages them, I'm sure of it. The first time the plumber came we really did have a legitimate problem. But since then, the pipes have been going crazy."

"Maybe he's a terrible plumber," I said.

"He fixes pipes in the best houses in town," said Roz. "Once he even worked in the governor's mansion. That's not in town, but the word gets around. He plumbs okay, but after he leaves, Gilda *un*-plumbs. I know it's love. He doesn't even come from Texas. He's from Aroostook County in Maine. Where the potatoes come from."

Gilda called to us, and we ran downstairs. She was standing at the foot of the stairs with a very worried look on her face. She said, "I don't think I should allow you two so far from home by yourselves. I just don't know. Maybe I'll keep you home with me."

"And the plumber," said Roz. Roz wasn't what I would call tactful. I knew she felt pretty desperate, because it wasn't her usual kind of remark.

Gilda just continued to stand there. She'd changed from watchdog to lovesick puppy. It was wonderfully romantic.

"You already promised us," said Roz.

Gilda grinned. "So I did. I never break a promise. Let's go."

"Did you order your necklace?" I asked as we drove along.

"Sure did. Not from that Miss Thistle though. She's out sick. If you ask me, she was *in* sick the other day. What a jittery soul."

"Sick?" said Roz. "Sick with what? Is it an illness kind of sick or is she hurt?"

"How should I know?" said Gilda. "Sick can mean spending an afternoon at the movies or visiting a friend or cleaning house. If people were more honest, sick would always mean sick, but it doesn't. Maybe she's out having her hair done. It was standing on end the other day. Did you notice?"

"What do you think?" Roz whispered to me.

But I had no chance to reply because Gilda drove up to the library.

"I'll pick you up in the best sellers between five and five-thirty," she said. "But don't hang out there."

"I can promise you we won't," said Roz.

Roz and I walked into the library. Then Roz stopped. "She must have driven away by now," she said. "Let's go *shopping*."

We walked out of the library. "Wait," said Roz. "We'd better leave a note so she won't worry

81

about us if we're not back on time. If we do get back here by five, we'll destroy the note. C'mon. To the best sellers." For the second time, Roz and I walked into the library. We wrote a note using Roz's pencil and paper.

Dear Gilda,
 Some people need all the help they can get. Remember the Alamo? But some people do better on their own. We are in the second group. Don't look for us. We will be safe. Most likely.
Love,
Rosalind and Anna

P. S. Also, we will be back for supper if supper is late and we will call you if we need a ride.

I took the most dust-free book I could find from the shelf and I put the note on page 165. I have a few favorite numbers. One hundred and sixty-five is one of them.

"What are you doing?" asked Roz.

"Watch and listen," I said. I walked up to a librarian at desk. "Excuse me, could you please hold this book for a lady who will come by between five and five-thirty? She'll have a loud voice and a lot of hair and teeth and she'll walk very fast and she'll be looking for two girls. She answers to the name of Gilda."

"Will she be checking out this book?" asked the librarian.

"That's up to her, but tell her to turn to page 165. There's a note for her there."

"Very well," said the librarian, and then she slowly printed a little note and put it in the book so that most of it stuck out like a marker. From what I could read upside down, she had printed "5–5:30, TONSILS, TRESSES, TEETH, GAIT, GIRLS, GILDA, 165." I think she was using some kind of word-association technique which I've read about and which works for educated people. I'm a believer in whole sentences myself.

"Why didn't you just give her the note?" whispered Roz.

"Notes in books have *authority*," I said. "The librarian might not want to be a note deliverer. But a note in a book — that's different. Let's go."

"Hurray, we're free," cried Roz as we walked away. "On to Wyman Brothers."

"Not so loud," I said. "On two counts. First count, we're in a library. Second count, I shouldn't have to tell you."

10

Outside the library I really felt free. "Talk, speak, yell," I said.

But Roz said quietly, "Let's go to the jewelry department first and check on why Miss Thistle is absent. Then we'll go the third floor."

"Okay, if it makes you feel better," I said. "You've shopped on the third floor, haven't you? Tell me about the layout."

"I've only been in certain sections," said Roz. "I usually go to the dress department. It's tremendous. In fact, there are dress departments within the dress department. I know there are offices down a corridor to the right of the elevator, but I've never been in them. Room 302 must be there."

It took us almost fifteen minutes to get to Wyman Brothers. We visited Longfellow's statue, which was out of our way, and Roz stopped to say a few words to him. Personally, I would never say a word to an inanimate object, but I have heard of people who regularly chat with paintings, automobiles, and houses.

At Wyman Brothers the 50th Anniversary celebration was still on. Another woman was in Miss Thistle's place in the jewelry department. "Pardon me, where is Miss Thistle?" I asked.

"She's out today," said the woman. "Need some help?"

"No, but is she out with anything special?"

"All I know is I was brought down from girdles to take her place today. Nobody told me nothing."

"Did Miss Thistle phone in herself, or did somebody phone in for her?" asked Roz.

"Like I said, I don't know nothing."

"Well, thank you anyway," said Roz.

"For nothing," I said.

"Look, I don't know from no phone calls. Girdles I know. Ask me about girdles. We've got a special up there today. Tell your mothers."

"Thanks again, Ida," said Roz. Ida's name was on her 50th Anniversary card.

We walked away. "Well, you learn something new with every experience," said Roz. "There's a special on girdles. I knew this was our day."

We took the elevator to the third floor. We stepped out into a world of hats and coats. "Dresses are to the left," said Roz. "Are we looking for Sabrina first?"

"We'll look for where the Sabrina Shop is going

to be. But I don't think Sabrina will be there yet. My guess is that she works in the promotion office with Sherman High, and on May 3rd he's promoting her, you might say."

We walked through Casual Dresses and Misses' Dresses up to Junior Dresses. Between Junior and Better Dresses there was a large open area, and workmen were moving around in it carrying boards, and sawing and hammering. There was a big sign.

PLEASE EXCUSE OUR APPEARANCE
BUT WE'RE GETTING READY
TO WELCOME SABRINA.
ON MAY 3 THE SABRINA SHOP
WILL OPEN HERE.

Roz and I wandered around, but all we could see were the workmen, and people watching the workmen. We walked into Better Dresses. A saleswoman who was so well-dressed that she turned Roz and me into instant hobos by comparison looked us over and then moved away. I have read that my age group was responsible for a high percentage of sales throughout the country, but this information obviously had not reached this saleswoman.

Roz and I didn't budge. At last the saleswoman came over and said, "Yes, miss?" Her voice was as well dressed as the rest of her, and it was phony. It was not the kind of voice she could call a dog with, or curse with, or order a hamburger with. But it was perfect for Better Dresses.

"What's the story on the Sabrina Shop?" I asked.

"The story, if you wish to put it that way, is that it will open May 3rd. The clothes it will carry will not be up to the quality found in Better Dresses, but they should be adequate for those people on *somewhat limited budgets*."

"I heard that Mr. Sherman High is the brains behind the idea," I said.

"Brains. How quaint," said the saleswoman. "He's the executive chiefly responsible for the Sabrina Shop. He's the one responsible for taking away, as of this moment, one fourth of Better Dresses as well as one fourth of Junior Dresses in order to create room for his Sabrina Shop. Every evening after the store closes, he and the Wyman brothers meet here, and the next day I find a little more of Better Dresses being carted away. It's like dying a little each day. One never knows what will be gone tomorrow."

Roz and I walked away. "Say, do you think she talks through her nose on purpose?" Roz asked.

"I don't care how she talks," I said. "It's what she talks about that counts. Like nightly meetings about the Sabrina Shop between Sherman High and the Wyman brothers. How would you like to attend a meeting? Well, not really attend. Observe would be more like it."

"After the store closes?" said Roz. "We'll have to hide, and sneak around, and Annie, are you sure we should?"

"Nope, but it's either that or use our invitation to meet Sherman High face to face. He'd probably be polite, and where would that get us? Criminals' manners, along with their clothes, are getting better and better. And that makes it harder and harder to catch them. Now are you with me?"

"I'm with you," said Roz.

"The time is now three-fifteen. The store closes at five-thirty. I saw signs saying so. From three-fifteen until five-twenty we can have a gay old time shopping. At five-twenty we hide. And we stay hidden. The store will close, the customers and salespeople will go home, and the meeting will begin. And we'll hear everything that's said."

"How can we if we hide in a dressing room?" asked Roz.

"Who said anything about hiding in a dressing room?"

"Isn't that where a person would hide? I mean, where else is there?"

"I have a glorious place picked out," I said. "Have you ever heard of the Trojan Horse?"

"Yuh, but somebody already thought of that a

long time ago and very far away. This is Wyman Brothers, Portland, Maine, and the time is *now*."

"Our Trojan Horse will be an iron horse — a train," I said. "Except it's made of cardboard or something. Come, I'll show you. It's in Junior Dresses."

When we had gone through the Junior Dress Department before, I had noticed a pink and red train about five feet long and three feet high and two feet wide. On one of the four sides it said ALL ABOARD FOR 50TH ANNIVERSARY BARGAINS, and on the opposite side it said FULL SPEED AHEAD ON OUR 50TH ANNIVERSARY SPECIAL. On one end there was a cardboardy door with a paper knob. I had given the knob a tiny tug as I went by, and the door had opened. I hadn't told Roz because she had only unkind words for vandal types. Now I told her.

Roz looked at the train and gave the knob a tiny pull, even though it was against her principles. She peeked inside.

I said, "It will be like having a cozy room to ourselves. On a train it's called a drawing room. How's that for elegant?"

"How's that for stuffy?" said Roz. "Whew!"

"The top has some open spaces in it," I said, "so we can breathe. But we'll have to stick close together and not raise our heads."

"How can we see what's going on?" asked Roz.

89

"We can! That's what makes it so ideal," I said. "Walk around the train. Try to be casual. You'll see that all the O's in the words on the train are holes. On one side ABOARD, FOR, and 50 all have O's. And on the other side ON OUR 50TH has O's. ON OUR 50TH faces the Sabrina section, so that's the side we'll look through, but the extra O's can also help us breathe."

"Speaking of aboard," said Roz, "how do we get aboard, or I should say inside, without being seen?"

"Luck will play a major part," I said. "At five-twenty we'll sort of hang around the area. When the coast is clear, and no one is looking, one of us will open the door and go in. Then when the coast is clear again, the other one of us will go in. The coast being clear is where the luck part comes in. Do you want to be first or second?"

"Want is not the right word," said Roz. "But I'll go first and get it over with. If we're caught, we can just say we were having fun, right?"

"Right. And now let's shop."

Roz and I tried on dresses, hats, coats, and wigs. We told ourselves we were serious about buying something. Otherwise all those try-ons wouldn't have been the sporting thing to do. Roz kept reminding me that whatever we bought would have to "go aboard," but I told her not to worry about it.

At five-twenty, without any luggage, we were back in Junior Dresses. It was so easy to get into the train undetected that it was actually disappointing. I would have been more disappointed if I had known the truth, which I found out later. The truth was that we *were* detected, but nobody cared. Kids, big kids, little kids, medium-size kids and an occasional peewee adult had discovered the train before me, and they had been in and out constantly since the time it was set up. In fact, the train was on its eighteenth paper doorknob so far. It had happened to be empty when I had seen it earlier in the afternoon, and it was empty again when Roz and I entered it. I also found out later that it was supposed to be checked every evening at closing time to make sure it was vacant, but the checker knew it was so uncomfortable and boring inside that nobody in his right mind would stay for more than a couple of minutes. So the checker didn't bother to check. I would have, if it had been my job. A trust is a trust.

Roz's athletic ability came in handy. She did some tricky things with her body, and settled in fast. I settled on my hands and knees. Roz stationed herself behind the O's in ON and OUR, and I used the O in 50TH. The first person in got two O's, the second got one. It was spaced that way. So Roz got the best view, but she deserved it.

Five-thirty seemed to take a long time to come.

A bell rang. Customers slowly left the floor. Sales-people slowly left. Everything seemed slow to us. Some lights went off, some stayed on, but it was bright around us. Roz and I kneeled and sat in different ways every few minutes. It was bearable inside the train, but barely bearable.

The Sabrina area was clear of workmen. They had left before the store closed. Suddenly three men appeared, walking together. They stopped in the middle of the area. I strained to see through my o. I recognized Nathan and Harry Wyman from their picture. The third man had a big round body and a small head. He looked like a snowman who had a good tailor. He said, "Sabrina will be here in a minute. Fred is bringing her. She's a gorgeous creature, she's a winner, I love her."

"I hope she's all you say she is, Sherman," said Harry Wyman.

"Sherman," Roz whispered to me.

"Sherman," I whispered back.

"Now what about Miss P.P.T.?" asked Nathan Wyman.

"Nobody wanted her," said Sherman High. "I have places where I can usually get rid of them, but she was much too out-of-date, and she couldn't just hang around the store taking up space for-ever. What choices did I have? I could have chopped her up and dumped her, that'd be the easiest, but ole Sherm's too tender-hearted for that. Know what I did?"

Nathan Wyman said what, Harry Wyman said what, Roz whispered what and so did I.

Even with four people wanting an answer, the question didn't get answered. Sherman boomed out, "Here's Fred and Sabrina! C'mon, baby, you gorgeous redhead, you."

Sherman reached out and hugged a red-headed young woman also being hugged by Fred. Yes, she was beautiful, even at a distance and seen through an o. She was beautiful and she was red-headed and she was made of plastic.

"A dummy!" said Roz. "Sabrina's a dummy."

"Yeah," I said. "That makes three of us."

11

If someone had walked by our hiding place, they would have heard the only gasping train in existence.

"I don't get it," said Roz. "Sabrina is a dummy. I don't think a dummy can replace a real person, so is Miss P.P.T. a dummy, too?"

"Hold on," I said. "We'll find out."

We continued to look through our o's. We watched Fred set up Sabrina. Then he disappeared, but he came back with another Sabrina, a sitting Sabrina (like Longfellow, but prettier). Then he went away again and came back. When he was finished going away and coming back, there were five Sabrinas — smiling, unsmiling, dreamy, bored, sitting, standing, etcetera, etcetera, etcetera. He placed them in different parts of the area.

"A Sabrina arena," I whispered to Roz.

"We'll rotate these," said Sherman High. "We'll probably have two on display at a time. Well, what do you think of her? We tried to make her look just like the newspaper drawings."

"And she does," said Harry Wyman. "It's remarkable. In my opinion, this shop will be a tremendous success." He turned to his brother. "Don't you think so?"

"No doubt about it," said Nathan Wyman.

"Glad you agree," said Sherman High. "When I dreamed up Sabrina for the newspaper ads, I didn't expect her to go into orbit. But she's a smash, sales are way up. This Sabrina Shop was the next logical step. Too bad we had to remove some 'Betters' and 'Juniors.' "

"Which reminds me," said Harry Wyman. "Are we going to remove any more fixtures from those departments?"

"We're about finished," said Sherman High. "Except for the temporary anniversary stuff like that train over there. That's grabbing loads of space. As soon as it goes, the Junior Department will open right into the Sabrina Shop. Fred and I can move the train now and show you the effect."

Roz kicked me. It wasn't easy to do inside the train. "We're going on a trip," she said. "You didn't tell me the train would be traveling."

Sherman High and Fred advanced toward the train.

Harry Wyman said, "I think we can visualize what you mean. Don't bother to move the train."

Roz whispered, "The trip's canceled, and three cheers for Harry Wyman."

But Nathan Wyman said, "I think we should see exactly what the space will look like without the train."

Roz whispered, "I liked Harry Wyman's idea better."

Through my O, I could see two pairs of legs, Sherman High's and Fred's. They were undecided legs. They moved toward us, stopped, then moved toward us again and stopped.

Fred said, "There's a chance that this train will collapse if we move it."

"There's a chance that I will, too," whispered Roz.

Nathan and Harry Wyman nodded to each other — sideways and up and down. I couldn't figure out what that meant. When people know each other very well, they sometimes use little signals that they can immediately translate, but which leave an outsider puzzled. Roz and I should have one. Kicking each other is much too common.

"Don't move the train," said Nathan Wyman.

"I second the motion," whispered Roz.

"You mean you second the non-motion," I said.

If Gilda were with us, she would have laughed. Gilda! I had forgotten about her.

"Gilda must be frantic by now," I said. "Even if she got our note."

"Oh, boy, I was so busy being frantic myself, I forgot about her," said Roz. "I bet our names and description are now known by every policeman in the city of Portland."

"Shh, they're talking again."

Nathan Wyman said, "Well, that takes care of everything except Miss P.P.T. What did you really do with her, Sherman? You've piqued our curiosity."

"Come to my office and I'll show you," said Sherman High. He grabbed one Sabrina, and started to walk away with her. "Fred, you take the other Sabrinas back for now."

The Wyman brothers and Sherman High and a smiling, vertical Sabrina left. Then Fred left with one Sabrina, came back and left with another Sabrina, came back, etcetera, etcetera, etcetera.

"After he takes the last Sabrina, let's get out of here," I whispered to Roz.

"You talked me into it. Whew!"

Fred left with Sabrina Number Five and turned out some lights. Roz and I scrambled out of the train.

"To Room 302 and hurry," I said.

"Who do you think I am," said Roz. "A taxi driver? What do we do when we get there?"

"We'll listen outside the room," I said.

"What if we can't hear?" said Roz.

"There you go, worrying in advance," I said.

"If we can't hear, we'll worry about it when we can't hear."

We rushed through Junior Dresses. In the middle of Misses' Dresses we heard a noise. Then we saw a flashlight coming our way. "It must be a store guard," I whispered. "Stand still. Freeze. Pretend you're a mannequin."

I had always wanted to try a graceful pose like a mannequin's, but it's silly to do it without a reason. I knew I would never have a better reason than now. I held up one hand and put the other on my hip. I tilted my head sideways. This was a typical mannequin pose, and it also gave me a chance to see what Roz was doing. She had frozen in front of a three-way mirror and was practicing a pose. Mannequins usually are not found in front of three-way mirrors, and in addition Roz had both arms raised as if someone had said, "Stick 'em up." But there was something original and touching about her pose. Maybe it would have worked if she hadn't moved one arm slightly just as the store guard appeared. Since she was at a three-way mirror, four arms moved. It was all over for Roz.

I was still standing there, and I mean still. I had a choice of giving myself up, or waiting until the guard took Roz away, and then getting help. What kind of help, I didn't know. My problem didn't last long. The guard said to Roz, "The mirror never lies, little lady. You look beautiful, all four of you. But isn't it a little dark to be admiring yourself? And your friend over there is gonna land up with a strained neck if she doesn't drop that swan act. What's going on here? You two shoplifters or something? You're mighty young to be starting on a life of crime."

"Shoplifters?" said Roz. "As it happens, we have a personal invitation from Mr. Nathan Wyman to come to the third floor whenever we're in the store. Well, this is whenever."

"A personal invitation," said the guard. "I suppose it's engraved and I suppose you left it at home."

"How did you know we left it at home?" asked Roz.

"Look, little lady, it's easier to tell a lie in the dark than in the daylight. Did you know that? But it's not any easier to *believe* the lie. And I don't believe a word you've said."

Roz was speechless. I said, "I guess you've heard a million stories, huh?"

"Yah, how did you know?" said the guard. "Some are worse than yours, what do you think of that? When I retire I'm gonna write a book about my experiences. That book's gonna make me rich. The cab drivers do it and make a mint."

"Well, here's something for your book," I said. "Our story is true. Take us to Room 302 and we'll prove it. Both Wyman brothers are there."

"Since I have to take you somewhere, okay," said the guard. "That'll be our first stop before I call the police."

It was showdown time. Now we would find out about Miss P.P.T. and meet Sherman High and the Wyman brothers. But they would also find out about us. It might not be an even exchange.

The guard knocked on the door of Room 302 although it was open. Then the three of us walked in. "Beg your pardon, sirs, but look what turned up hiding in Misses' Dresses. They claim they have a personal invitation from you to come to the third floor whenever they're in the store. That's their story. It's my duty to repeat it."

"They must have received Form Letter Number 8," said Nathan Wyman, "which invites interested customers to visit our store. However, that does not mean after hours. Thank you, guard. We'll take over from here."

The guard absolutely smirked at Roz and me. Some people are disgusting in victory. He left, whistling and twirling his flashlight like a baton.

"Girls, this is my brother Mr. Harry Wyman," said Nathan Wyman, "and this is Mr. Sherman High, our promotion manager. Now who are you? Why were you hiding in the dark? Do your parents know you're here? What are your names?"

"I'm Anna and she's Rosalind," I said. "I can't tell you my last name. My mother has a rule about that. I live in New York. My mother knows I'm in Portland, Maine, but she doesn't know exactly where I am from hour to hour."

"I can't tell you my last name either," said Roz. "My friend's mother has a rule about that. My mother is in Bangor, Maine, but she doesn't know exactly where I am from hour to hour."

"Let's try another approach," said Harry Wyman. "Do you have a rule about your telephone number?"

Roz looked at me. I shook my head no.

"No rule about that," said Roz. "But sometimes I forget mine. I know it's something like 722–0548, but it could also be 722–0584 or maybe 722–0458. I have trouble that way. Isn't that called transposition? I mean, like if you were called Wyman Harry. Know what I mean?"

"We know," said Harry Wyman. "Let's assume for a moment that *your* name was transposed. Your last name would then be Rosalind. What would your first name be?"

"It would be the name I can't tell you," said Roz.

"We are getting nowhere," said Sherman High. "Suppose we stop asking questions, and you girls simply give us answers. Say whatever you like, but include the reason why you were hiding in the store."

"We've got a good reason for that," I said. I turned to Roz. "I'm going to tell everything. It's now or never."

I began my story.

"See, Roz here is my best friend and she used to live in New York. Well, as I mentioned, I live in New York. Well, Roz invited me to visit her and naturally I accepted and I took a plane last Sunday and — "

When I started my story, everybody was standing, but one by one we sat down. Only Sabrina was left standing, but she had no choice. I told everything, including that we had first seen the Sabrina ad in a fish kitchen.

I ended my story, "And so here we are."

"And here I am," said Sherman High. "The arch villian. Oh, baby, what a story. I'm no murderer, kids, but with your abilities, *you* could land in jail." He took out a cigar and laughed. "So you're the one who took my suitcase. Well, at least you returned it. I didn't even know Miss Thistle was on that flight. Miss Thistle's got a way of shrinking to a fraction of her size. And I've got more news for you. Miss P.P.T. is a mannequin, not a person. A mannequin is a dummy, by the way."

Sherman High puffed on his cigar. He seemed

very pleased with himself. He didn't remind me of a snowman any more. A snowman can only melt, but he seemed to be inflating.

"My friend Anna has known what a mannequin is practically since the day she was born," said Roz. "But what we don't know is why the mannequin has Miss Thistle's initials. And you haven't told us."

Sherman High had a problem with Roz that he didn't know about. His problem was that he was the complete opposite of a stray cat or a wounded bird.

He took another puff on his cigar. "Miss Thistle has worked for Wyman Brothers for many years, mainly in Better Dresses. Several years ago, we got in a new mannequin for that department. This mannequin happened to look like a younger version of Miss Thistle, and Miss Thistle took a real shine to her, as if she had invented her. Somebody started to call the mannequin Miss P.P.T. and the name stuck. Miss Thistle began to fuss over the mannequin, always straightening out its clothes and calling the customer's attention to whatever it was wearing, and ignoring the other clothes in the department. So finally we had to transfer Miss Thistle out of the department. We put her in jewelry. But she continued to visit her namesake in Better Dresses almost every lunch hour. You know, some people feed pigeons, some people walk the streets, some people visit mannequins. Live and let live."

He looked at Nathan and Harry Wyman. They nodded.

"So why did you have to get rid of Miss P.P.T.?" asked Roz.

Sherman puffed in Roz's direction. "When I started preparing for the Sabrina Shop, part of Better Dresses had to go, and Miss P.P.T. was included. She was out-of-date, stodgy. That's when I wrote the memo to my staff. When Miss Thistle got wind of it, she was horrified. Well, she was always horrified, but this time she was doubly horrified." Sherman High puffed again in Roz's direction. "Well, ole Sherm came up with a fabulous idea. Are you ready for this? Miss Thistle is now the proud owner of Miss P.P.T."

He took a piece of paper from a desk drawer. "Here's the new memo I wrote." He passed it around the room.

Memo from S.H.
_____

Give Miss P.P.T. to Miss P.P.T.
Make all necessary arrangements

104

"Today was the big day. I even gave Miss Thistle the day off to accept delivery and settle Miss P.P.T. into her place. She phoned this afternoon to say she feels like a new person, she feels so *secure*. She put Miss P.P.T. near a window, so it will always appear that someone is home. 'Very discouraging to robbers,' Miss Thistle said."

Sherman High settled back in his chair. "That's ole Sherm's idea of a happy ending." He puffed. He yawned. I yawned, too. It felt like two o'clock in the morning after a party. I had been to a couple that late. Nathan and Harry Wyman had sat quietly through both stories, looking amused and pleased. Sherman High and I had probably been more entertaining than what they would have found on television that night, since Portland is only a four-channel city.

"Here they are! Here they are!" I heard a woman's voice screech. The guard came rushing in. This time he didn't bother to knock. I could see why. Tramping behind him, almost on top of him, was Gilda. And right behind her was a red-faced man in dark gray coveralls.

"You girls," said Gilda. "Is this what you call the public library? It's lucky for you that the librarian heard you say you were going to Wyman Brothers. Otherwise I would have called the police. What are you doing here?"

"We are having a story-swapping session," said Sherman High, "and it was a beaut. Too bad you missed it. My name is Sherman High and this is Mr. Harry and Mr. Nathan Wyman. Looks like you already know the girls."

Gilda took one step backward. "*The* Wyman brothers? Well, well, well. My name is Gilda and this is Byron. We've come to take the girls home. Right now."

Byron beamed. I liked his gray coveralls. They were functional, which is a vital part of good design, and they were well tailored, for coveralls. On the breast pocket there was an emblem of crossed pipes and the words PLUMB GOOD PLUMBERS INC.

Gilda seemed about to grab Roz, but Roz was already moving toward the door. "Thanks ever so much for your hospitality." Roz smiled at the Wyman brothers and Sherman High. It wasn't really the right thing to say and it wasn't really the wrong thing. But it got us politely out the door.

12

We went home in Byron's truck. That's how Gilda and Byron had gotten to the library and to Wyman Brothers. On the way home Gilda told us that if we promised "never to do anything so harebrained again" she wouldn't tell Roz's father what had happened. We promised. I was very surprised that Gilda wasn't prying into what we had been doing at Wyman Brothers. For someone who was a veteran looker through other people's envelopes, it seemed amazing. But it didn't seem amazing for long. Gilda had other things on her mind.

"Byron, you keep your eyes on the road, and I'll tell them the news," she said.

I think Byron beamed, but I was sitting in the back so I couldn't be sure.

"Byron and I are engaged."

"You're what?" said Roz.

"Engaged," said Gilda. She held out her third finger, left hand. It was bare. "This is where the ring will go when I get it. Oh, and the pipes are shipshape now."

"Best wishes to both of you," I said.

I think that Byron beamed again.

Roz looked as if she were going to cry. Suddenly I knew she would miss Gilda. Now Roz wouldn't have anybody to try to get away from. It would be lonely, and perfect pipes wouldn't be any consolation.

"Your family doesn't need me any more," Gilda said to Roz. "You're at the age where you can be a real help to your mother. I'll tell her so when she comes back from Bangor. Fact is, you haven't needed me for a long time. Byron needs me."

Roz still looked as if she were going to cry.

We beat Roz's father home by about five minutes. Of course he didn't know he was in a race. Gilda had telephoned him from the library that there would be a "slight delay" for supper, so he had stayed on at his office to finish some work. Roz's father told Byron that he was "a lucky guy" to be getting Gilda. Gilda said that she was "a lucky girl." That remark finally placed her in the girl category, but she was the placer so it didn't count.

Byron stayed on for supper. It tasted absolutely awful. It was Gilda's first food flop since I had been visiting. I think the food was grounds for Byron's breaking the engagement, but he said everything was delicious and he asked for seconds. He told Roz's father that the pipes were now in topnotch condition and that he didn't expect any future trouble and that there would be no bill.

Roz and I excused ourselves after supper and went up to her room. It was our first chance to be alone since the guard had caught us.

"I'm confused," said Roz. "How could we have thought that Sherman High might be a murderer?"

"We put two and two together and unfortunately we got five for an answer," I said. "In fact, not only isn't he a murderer, he's almost a hero. He helped Miss Thistle feel safer, and that's practically a prize-winning accomplishment."

Roz was quiet for a long time. Then she said, "I'm glad Gilda doesn't know what we did. She might think I'm awful."

"She'd never think that," I said. "And why should you care what Gilda thinks? She might be the strictest person going, but she's not strict about herself. She breaks pipes and she tries to read other people's mail."

Roz said, "She took care of me just the same."

Roz was right. Gilda *had* taken care of her in her own style. I guess her intentions were A number 1, but her actions sometimes hit rock bottom.

Maybe it's possible to be two different persons in one. Who knows, maybe if I really looked for it, when I got back to New York I could find Slugger Schultz's other person.

Actually, Roz and I were much further from perfect than I had originally thought, and I knew we would never qualify for any good-behavior medals.

"Well, at least you were right about the Wyman brothers," said Roz. "Aren't they nice? They didn't even make us promise not to hide out in their store any more."

"That reminds me," I said. "I promised to call home."

My mother answered the telephone. She asked me what I'd been doing, and I said, "This and that." I told her that Gilda was engaged and she asked, "Nice fellow?" and I said yes and she asked, "From Texas?" and I said no. Then my mother gave me the latest installment on the actress. The tickets had arrived, and there were three of them. Twelfth-row center. For next Tuesday. Which reminded my mother that I was coming home Sunday. She said she and my father would meet me at the airport and told me to have a pleasant trip. Then my father got on to say that he'd see me on Sunday, Sugar. I said, "See you Sunday" and I hung up.

"Only two more days left," said Roz. "And you haven't even seen Portland Headlight, our famous lighthouse on the cape. The one on a trillion postcards. And I haven't made your perfume yet. And all kinds of things."

For the next two days Roz and I went sightseeing and shopping. With Gilda. And Byron. He had quit his job, and they were planning to move upstate to Aroostook County to live on a potato farm. They were getting married in Roz's house as soon as Roz's mother returned. "Too bad you'll miss the ceremony," Gilda said to me. It *was* too bad.

We did some of our shopping at Wyman Brothers, naturally. Maybe it was my imagination, but Roz seemed to be hanging onto Gilda now. Wherever Gilda went, Roz followed. And so I did, too. We went to the third floor. The Sabrina Shop was shaping up, and the anniversary train was doing good business. Downstairs, I stopped to say goodby to Miss Thistle. I told her I'd come by the next time I was in Portland. She didn't ask how I was getting back to New York, and I didn't tell her. I also didn't mention Miss P.P.T. I felt that Miss Thistle was entitled to the roommate of her choice, but it would have been embarrassing to ask, "How's your roommate?" in a situation like hers.

On Sunday morning Roz, her father, Gilda, and I were at the airport, and the visit was over. "Now you're going your way and I'm going mine," said Roz. "We're like Longfellow wrote, like 'ships that pass in the night.' "

"No, we're not," I said. "His ships never got together. That's not us. And besides, we'll both be going in the same direction again. You're visiting me this summer. That's definite."

I checked in my suitcase. The smiling man wasn't there, but another smiling man was. "Never throw away your suitcase," said Roz, "even if it falls apart."

At a gift counter I bought a plastic napkin holder with a picture of Portland Headlight for my parents. Then it was time to board the plane. Suddenly I was remembering what I hadn't done in Portland. I hadn't helped Gilda with the dishes, I hadn't told Roz about the new teacher at school, I hadn't smelled the perfume she was making for me. But the hads outnumbered the hadn'ts about one hundred to one.

People around us were kissing and saying goodby and write and I'll be seeing you, and we were doing the same. I told Roz that I would see her in seventy-eight days. I had figured it out the night before. I wished Gilda happy times on her potato farm. "Byron would have been here," she said, "but he sleeps late Sundays."

I walked up into the plane. I found a seat by myself next to a window and looked out. They were all waving. I waved back, and kept waving until the plane took off.

Soon I was high in the sky, heading home.

About the Author

MARJORIE WEINMAN SHARMAT has published over ninety books for children and young adults, among them *Rich Mitch*, *Nate the Great*, *Getting Something on Maggie Marmelstein*, and *The Lancelot Closes at Five*.

Ms. Sharmat knows what it's like to go home with the wrong suitcase. One of her bags once wound up on someone else's honeymoon!

The author lives in Tuscon, Arizona, with her husband, Mitchell, who is also a children's book author. They have two grown sons.